TIME CHALLENGED

TIME CHALLENGED

Barbara Kennedy

ISBN: 979-8-9865685-7-7

EISBN: 979-8-9865685-6-0

This is a work of fiction, although some of the places are real.

CHAPTER 1

PETER HAD BEEN AT Toby's Tavern for half an hour. He was tired of standing and finally moved into the only seat available, which was across from a woman sitting alone in a small corner booth. She began talking as soon as he sat down.

"Timing is everything, and I don't have any," she said.

"What?" he asked.

"You know, it's all in the timing."

"I'm still not following you."

"Remember the llama craze? I missed it. Buy high, sell low, that's me. Remember the tech bubble?"

"Yeah," he responded tentatively.

"My bubble bottle didn't have a blower."

"Ah…what?" He smiled; insanity could be diverting.

"You know, one of those wand things—they come inside the bubble bottle, and you blow on them to make the bubbles. I have no sense of timing. I missed hula hoops and poodle skirts."

He looked at the woman sitting across from him. She had shoulder-length reddish-blond hair and very green eyes. He couldn't assess her figure while she was sitting down, but she was small, maybe five feet, four inches tall. He tried to gauge her age. With women it was hard to guess, but he figured early thirties.

"You weren't born yet," he pointed out.

"But I missed them." She paused to take a deep breath. "And I missed the green hair revolution."

"It was blue, and you were too old for that."

"Yeah, it just passed me by. And I missed the tattoo craze."

He couldn't help smiling at her absurd monologue nor could he resist responding. "You could still—"

"No, no! If I were to get a tattoo now, the entire tattoo industry would go out of business. I'm curvy, when straight up and down is in fashion. I'm a blond, when brunettes are in. I'm a redhead, when blonds are hot." She leaned across the table, inadvertently exposing surprisingly sensational cleavage. "See what I mean? No sense of timing." She sat back and drew a breath, but then another example of her appalling lack of timing struck her. "I am never eligible for any of those class action lawsuits advertised on television."

"OK, OK, I get it," Peter said, interrupting her. "You better stop now because you are starting to sound crazy, and crazy is definitely in, if you can get diagnosed as manic-depressive."

"No, no, that's been changed to bipolar or seasonally reactive. I missed that too."

One thing for certain was that she was challenging his

sense of timing. "Of all the bars in all the towns, I had to choose this one."

"Oh, that is a wonderful quote." She lit up with a dazzling smile. "You haven't got it quite right, but I recognize it. *Casablanca*, right?"

She was decidedly tipsy, and she was definitely *not* his responsibility…

"What are you doing here all alone?" he asked. She certainly should not be alone in her current condition.

"I am waiting for a friend. But she called a little while ago. She has to work late—well, had to work late—to cover a shift. You know, the hospital is short of nurses. See what I mean? Bad timing."

"You should have known that your friend was going to have to work late," he said.

"No, no, that's too much to ask of the time challenged. But I should have gone home when she called."

"When did she call?"

"A little while ago," she answered vaguely.

"Your sense of timing may be a bit off," he agreed.

Toby's was a tavern. It served outstanding seafood, but first and foremost, it was a tavern. It was always crowded on Friday nights, but there were few choices in the small waterfront town of Coupeville, Washington. Peter's sister, Kat, promised to meet him there an hour ago. As usual, she was late and not answering her cell phone, if it was even turned on. He tried the beach house number, and there was no answer there either. He should have known better. He should have just driven on to the beach house, but he figured they could share diner first since Kat did not cook.

"Exactly," she responded, bringing his focus back to the woman across the table. "Bad timing." Peter figured his timing might be a bit off tonight. He couldn't find his sister, and now he had another woman to worry about. Maybe if he fed her, she would sober up a little.

"How about some halibut and chips?"

"OK, but I mostly need another beer."

Peter signaled to the waitress as she passed. The beers were on the table long before the food. Eating didn't help much to sober up his self-described time-challenged companion.

Clair rarely drank, but tonight was an exception. She had been mentally reviewing her life.

Her grandmother died two years ago, leaving her beach cottage to her only child, Clair's mother. "A bolt-hole," her will designated it. Her mother divorced her father and moved into the beach property. She spent a year adding onto it and remodeling it. Last year, she decided that she wanted to go back to university for her master's degree. At the time, Clair was working as a research assistant in the history department at the University of Washington. She lived in a large two-bedroom apartment, also a legacy from her maternal grandparents. Her grandfather served as dean of the English department at one time. They actually owned a house in the university district. The house was divided into two apartments. Her mother thought she would simply move in with Clair and pursue her master's degree. As usual, given her time-challenged proclivity, this came at a time in Clair's life when she had reached her limit with the politics and backstabbing in the history department. She was seriously looking for a life change, but she wasn't excited about being college roommates with her mother.

Now she felt trapped in a tide pool and was feeling a little sorry for herself.

Her somewhat-maudlin life review was interrupted by the arrival of a large man who seated himself in her booth and proceeded to take charge in an obnoxiously male manner. She found herself with a third beer and a plate of halibut and chips in front of her.

"You, on the other hand, have excellent timing," Clair accused the male sitting across her.

"How do you know?"

"Oh, we who are time challenged can always recognize our opposites."

Peter wanted to deny it, but she was actually right. He was usually at the right place at the right time, and his life and finances had certainly benefited from it. The exception was his relationships with women—his excellent timing hadn't helped him much there. But he figured that was due to the women's poor timing.

"I suppose if we are going to exchange personal attributes, we should introduce ourselves. I'm Peter." He started to reach across the table and offer his hand but decided to offer neither his hand nor his last name to this confused female. He watched her tilt her head to one side and consider him.

"Clair," she responded guardedly. "Excuse me."

She rose from her seat and made her way through the crowded tavern to the inevitable and never-ending line for the women's bathroom. There was, of course, no line for the men's facilities. A few women were brave enough to break out of the line and use the men's room.

All the beer in my body urged me to find a bathroom in a timely manner. I finally broke from the line and followed the example of my braver sisters. My timing was lousy. Coming out of the men's room, I walked directly into the man who had been sitting with me for the past half hour. A six-feet-two wall of male muscle stood directly outside the door as I exited the men's room. He looked at the sign above the door that emphatically stated "men" and then turned his deep-blue eyes to me. If I made my move to use the men's room earlier, I would have missed this embarrassing encounter. But I am time challenged.

I returned to the table, left money to pay for my share of the meal, and pushed my way through the incoming tide of people and out the front door. My untimely trip to the men's restroom sobered me up enough to know that it was past time to "get out of Dodge," as they say. I cleared the doorway and had almost broken out of the surging, incoming press of would-be Friday night tavern patrons when I felt the slight pressure of a hand under my left elbow. I didn't have to look up to see the deep-blue eyes of the man I had just totally embarrassed myself in front of. I was still under the influence enough to realize that I was babbling about who knows what to this man for the past half hour—not to mention the little restroom incident.

"Ready?" he asked in a deep, disturbingly steady voice, as if we were actually together for the evening and naturally proceeding onto the next phase.

"When a man asks a woman if she is ready, what he really means is that *he* is ready."

"I am going to disregard that disparaging comment about my sex and drive you home."

"No, thank you. I am going to drive myself home. Loved sharing a booth and a bathroom with you." I tossed the exit line over my shoulder as I walked away from him.

For once, the gods of good timing smiled on me. I would never have been able to escape that particular male on my own. It wasn't that he was particularly interested in me, but he felt responsible. His honor impelled him to see my slightly inebriated self safely home. Ugh! These insights came to me clearly, and I knew that my leaving was timely. Fortunately, another woman interceded. I looked back over my shoulder and saw him in conversation with a small, slender woman in a long skirt and a lavender hooded sweatshirt. She had light-brown, short, spiked hair, and I almost walked into a lamppost trying to see more. Luckily, my friend Shannon pulled into the parking area just as I found my car. She apologized for her late arrival and insisted on driving me home.

Could it be that my timing was improving?

CHAPTER 2

"YOU'RE EARLY," IRIS SNARLED at me as she unlocked the gate to the nursery driveway. It was Iris's nature to be surly, so it wouldn't have mattered what time I arrived. I worked weekends at the Rosehip Nursery, owned and mostly operated by Iris and her partner, Lisa. The nursery had grown so fast the past two years that they needed help on the weekends. That was me, weekend help.

"And a good Saturday morning to you too," I answered Iris.

I was feeling anything but cheerful myself this morning. I totally erased last night from my mind and memory, but my body was not as forgiving. Luckily, Lisa was feeling friendly, so I didn't have to deal with the public. Instead, I labored hard, weeding and mulching a large vegetable plot, under the occasional supervision of an old golden Labrador and a large orange cat. August could actually get hot on the island, and by lunchtime I sweated out all the accumulated alcohol from my body. The three of us shared tuna sandwiches on the back porch of the shop, interrupted periodically by customers. It was a good workday, and I was pleasantly tired when I left and headed home. Sunday was a little slower, and I had to work in the shop, but all in all, the weekend leveled me out from my rocky Friday night low.

Monday was a dead day in Coupeville, so it was my day off. It was a gorgeous day, and I decided to go for a walk. I could always do my laundry later. It wasn't like I had a social life. I walked up the trail through the woods and headed toward the old pheasant farm. I knew I couldn't get into the farm area itself, but I liked to walk around the edges. I was thrilled when I found the back gate hanging open. I had heard that the state was going to sell the farm. The birds had been gone for months. Everyone in the area was hoping that the land wouldn't go to a developer. Mom said that she heard a nature conservatory was interested. I always wanted to explore the area, wanted to search for the perfect feather. I liked to use feathers for bookmarks.

The open gate invited me into the netted area, and one fenced pen led to another. It was just too great an opportunity to pass up. I planned to explore only the sections closest to the gate, but each new area opened ahead, drawing me in deeper and moving me farther away from the back entrance. The next area would certainly have the most perfect feather. I wandered on, heedless of any need for an exit. I was deep into a wild, fenced meadow when my body registered fatigue.

But it was such a long way back; maybe if I went on, I would find a break in the fence, a way out. The weeds and grasses were getting waist high, and it was slow going. There were masses of large thistles and wild blackberry bushes. From a distance, it looked as if there was no fencing between the posts in the area just ahead. I was tricked into moving toward it, only to find that the fence mesh was intact. I was hot and thirsty, and my legs were feeling heavy. I didn't have a watch on, but I felt as if I had been searching for a way out for hours. I worked my way up to the front section where the fence bordered the road. I wondered if the pheasants felt this way, if they thought that freedom was only another field away—that if they could just make it through to the next fence, there would surely be a small tear in the fencing, just big enough to slip through.

Finally, I saw the way out. There were no birds now, but I closed each gate carefully as I passed through the separate areas. Yes! I was through the last gate and onto the closely mown lawn surrounding the house. I looked up, planning to walk nonchalantly down the gravel driveway out to the road, when I almost walked right into him.

"Oh dear. Caught! Mr. McGregor, I presume? I hoped to sneak out!" I exclaimed.

"The way you sneaked in?" His deep voice cut off my explanation.

"Well, I am terribly sorry…you see, all the connecting gates were open, and they just kept leading me on—"

I was interrupted by what could only be described as a snort coming from the large man who blocked my way out. Oh no, it couldn't be. I remembered that voice. Damn my timing. It was the man from Toby's Tavern. Maybe he wouldn't recognize me. He glared down at me. I would just have to be brazen about it and pretend like I didn't recognize him.

"Oh well, what will it be, then? Pistols at dawn, or shall you simply draw and quarter me?" I asked.

The edges of his generous mouth might have lifted just the smallest fraction, but he didn't move an inch out of my way. I tried another tack.

"I've been wounded. Does that ameliorate my sin?"

"A little," he responded as I held out my left forearm, turning it to show him the deep, ugly scratch running from the elbow bend down to my wrist.

As I leaned forward slightly, three pheasant feathers fell out of my pocket. Damn. I saw his eyes move instantly to the incriminating evidence.

"I have paid a high price for those; I was savagely attacked by blackberry bushes." I began showing him another ugly gash just above my ankle.

"Not high enough," he answered.

"Oh, you are bloodthirsty."

"And you are on private property."

"Yes, well, there were no signs, but I *do* apologize. I knew I was trespassing."

I moved to the right, planning to walk around him. But he moved to block me. Despite his size and obvious strength, I was not afraid of him. I looked up, met his deep-blue eyes, and knew that he recognized me and had recognized me from the start of our conversation. I couldn't seem to stop my semihysterical babble...

"Would you like my head mounted on a pike to warn

off other would-be trespassers?"

"I'm considering it."

I moved to the left, trying to get around the man mountain, but he moved in front of me again.

"I am really very tired. Just what would you consider adequate restitution for my heinous crime?"

He raised an eyebrow and looked me over as though he might be considering a low bid at a used furniture auction. His gaze made me uncomfortably aware of my appearance. I knew my hair was a wild tangle of frizzy curls. I had not bothered with makeup. I hadn't planned on meeting anyone. My favorite green-and-brown-striped midcalf cotton pants had small holes in several places and were less than flattering. My sage-green T-shirt had three colors of paint on it from my bedroom walls. Instead of washing out, the paint set in permanently. The dark-green socks and old, scuffed Asics had nothing to recommend me, either. I wondered if my five feet three height could possibly feel any smaller. I was tired and running out of banter.

And then he moved out of my way like a predator that wasn't really hungry and lost interest in playing with his prey.

I walked quickly across the lawn and over the gravel drive to the road. I wasn't going to look back. I wasn't going to give him any opportunity to change his mind. But, of course, my terrible timing asserted itself, and I had to look back. I saw the small, brown-haired woman from Friday night join him on the driveway. *Oh, I am going to be a good little rabbit from now on*, I promised myself. No more drinking and no more trespassing.

"Who was that?" Kat asked.

"Just someone walking around the property."

"Do you think she is interested in buying?"

"No," Peter responded assuredly.

"Well, what do you think? Wouldn't it be perfect?" For the past hour, his sister kept asking him this question.

"Kat, it's a big investment. It would take a lot of work to repair all the fencing and build the kennels. Are you sure you feel up to it?"

"Marla is going to help me with the dogs."

"Yes, but you will need someone to oversee all the improvements and then manage the property. The outside areas have to be continually mowed, the fences need repair, and the kennels will have to be cleaned."

Peter envisioned the enormous amount of work and expense inherent in the purchase of the property and the pursuit of setting up a breeding kennel for Doberman pinschers. It was a huge property, but maybe if he could find the right manager, part of it could be used for boarding. That just might make it at least break even on expenses.

It wasn't the money, not really. After their parents died, he set up a trust fund for his sister. She had always been fragile. Growing up, she had asthma and every allergy known to man. She tried to go to college and was misdiagnosed with fibromyalgia. This was the first time he saw her excited since their parents died five years before. If it made her this happy, Peter would make it happen. He wasn't sure about her friend Marla. For the past year, Katelyn had been going to dog shows and visiting breeders with her. Peter had the woman investigated and couldn't find anything criminal in her background, but he worried about someone taking advantage of his very vulnerable sister.

He needed to find a strong, reliable manager to oversee this whole thing. Kat was looking pleadingly at him.

"All right, I'll talk to the realtor."

"Oh, Peter, you are the best of brothers." She threw herself into his arms.

CHAPTER 3

"YOU'RE LATE." TRUE, I was time challenged, but Sadie's accusation was invalid.

"I'm not late; it isn't even 5:30 a.m." Tuesday through Friday, I worked at the Sadie, Sadie Tried Lady Bakery located on the main street of Coupeville. My first job was to pick up the owner on the way to the bakery. Sadie was eighty years old, and although she had a restricted driver's license that allowed her to drive from home to work, both the Coupeville police and I felt it was better if Sadie was the passenger, rather than the driver, in any moving vehicle.

We started with the bakery's signature cinnamon rolls. The bakery opened at eight o'clock in the morning, and they would usually be gone half an hour later. Then we moved on to blueberry and pumpkin muffins and, since it was August on the island, blackberry cobbler. Sadie decided on oatmeal and basic white for the week's bread offerings and peanut butter and sugar cookies in the shape of maple leaves. The bakery did not take orders. It was strictly first come, first served, and what was on offer varied according to Sadie's whim of the week. It used to be her whim of the day, but when I took over buying the ingredients, she agreed to make the selections last an entire week. We also hired Tina, a part-time dishwasher, counter moneychanger, and general cleaner upper.

I loved the bakery in the early mornings before the customers arrived. Sadie was full of energy for the first few hours. She mixed and baked like a demon, but by 11:30 a.m., she was fading. I fed her lunch with a strong cup of tea, settled her at a table, and gave her invoices to sign. Tina came in at 12:30 p.m. She covered the counter and started on the washing up. I drove Sadie home for a nap. We closed the bakery at 2:00 p.m. On Fridays we were open for lunch. The menu varied according to what we had left over from the week. I started the lunch thing to use up the leftover baked goods from the week. We began with bread puddings and open-faced sandwiches, and then we added salads and soups. Sadie was OK with it, but she went home early on Fridays. On Fridays, Tina came in at 10:00 a.m. and drove Sadie home.

By the time she returned to wait tables and cover the counter, the bakery was full. Our four tables were continually occupied, and there was usually a line snaking out onto the porch. Tina was in charge of any leftover food after Friday lunch. She always seemed to know who needed a little extra food. Mrs. Owens always got at least a loaf of bread, and Mr. Mallory got two cinnamon rolls or a fruit tart and half a dozen cookies. Tina's neighbors, the Larsons, had five kids, and they could absorb any amount of leftover baked goods.

Despite the pleas from restaurants and individuals, these were our only standing orders, and we didn't earn a penny from them.

The bakery had a standing weekly bulk order from a supply company out of Seattle, so the basics came by truck every Monday morning. But the extras I bought locally. Sometimes I drove into Oak Harbor, but I frequently shopped for both myself and the bakery at the Prairie Center Mart, which was about ten miles from my beach cottage. It was located in the middle of several large farms and was a combined hardware and food provider for the area's rural families. It was closer than driving into town, which would have taken about forty-five minutes each way.

When I drove into the parking area, there were the requisite number of pickup trucks waiting for their loads and the smell of cow from the fields around the store. I was relieved that I didn't see anyone I knew in the store. I was feeling somewhat antisocial. It is a common feeling for those of us who are time challenged. We simply don't seem to be in the same time zone as others around us at any given moment.

My shopping was almost complete. The cart was full. I decided to go back for a large bag of birdseed. A rogue pheasant had been hanging around the cottage. He was probably an escapee from the bird farm. He was a handsome fellow, and I wanted him to stick around. He was brightly colored, so he was certainly a male. I couldn't offer him power or sex, so it would have to be food. In my experience, only one of those three things appealed to males of any species. I focused on the exact location of the birdfeed in the store.

Making a turn by produce and cutting the corner on the adjoining isle, I ran directly into a cart coming the other way.

"I'm sorry," I stammered, without looking up at the person behind the other cart. I tried to move my cart to the side just as he moved his in the same direction. Further flustered, I looked up into an amused pair of dark-blue eyes, the eyebrows just slightly raised, as though their owner was bemused by the situation. No, no, it couldn't be him. But it was. Even for the time challenged, this was too much. It was the same male; the one from Toby's and the one from the bird farm, my bête noire. His dark-brown hair tumbled down onto his forehead; the beginning of a smile was starting at the corners of his mouth. He looked totally out of place in the middle of a grocery store aisle. He also looked as if he might start a conversation.

"Are you always such a reckless driver?" His voice was low and surprisingly pleasant, with a touch of humor that was reflected in his face. I groaned.

"I think we have already done this scene," I said.

"Ah, the trespasser. Yes, the choreography is reminiscent."

"Yup, inebriant, trespasser, and reckless driver. You've certainly seen me at my shining best."

"Nice running into you," he quipped as I wrenched my full cart around his and hurled it in the opposite direction, skipping the birdseed. The male pheasant would not be pleased. I went right to the checkout counter as if I were being pursued, which I wasn't.

What a dolt I am, I castigated myself all the way back to the cottage. I relived my socially inept conversation and behavior, thinking of all the ways I could have dealt with the situation more appropriately. I was brilliant, I was witty, I was graceful, and I was in another time and place, as usual. What I was really upset about was the fact that I'd failed to gather any valuable information. I needed to know if he was going to be in my area of operation much longer. How was he connected to the old bird farm? I feared that he just might possibly be the new lord of the manor. That was a threatening thought for me, so I pushed it into another dimension of time.

Fall was coming, and I needed to find another job. The nursery would be going fallow for the fall and winter. It didn't pay much, anyway, but I always had fresh fruit and vegetables. After the apple harvest, the rain and the fog would settle in on the island. The heating bill would go up. I was helping Mr. Jenson occasionally in his antiques and bookstore. I did book searches for him online. Research was my thing, and he could easily offer a finder service if he hired me. I thought that there was a large enough retired and diversely esoteric population on the island to support the service. I needed to approach him with the suggestion. Of course, the timing might not be exactly right.

Peter pushed the loaded grocery cart down the narrow aisle of Prairie Center Mart. As usual, there was no food in the beach house kitchen. Kat was simply not interested in food. He decided that he would take two weeks off from work to assess her new project and make a decision about purchasing the old bird farm property. That meant he had to have sustenance. Kat would eat some of the food he put in front of her, and he had needs. He had a list—he functioned best when working from a list. He probably should have made the drive into Oak Harbor; there were several large grocery stores there. He would have had more selection, but he was meeting with the realtor this afternoon and didn't want to take the time.

He also needed to get his security retainer team to do in-depth research on Kat's prospective dog-breeding partner. The preliminary report hadn't turned up anything. But if Kat was going into business with this woman, he wanted a full investigation.

He used a shopping service for his own apartment in Seattle, so food shopping was unfamiliar territory for him in several ways. He was advancing with purpose toward the produce section when the collision occurred. He was willing to confess that he might have been at least partly at fault—he was looking at his list. That is, he was willing to admit partial culpability until he looked at the person behind the other cart. Oh no, it was that time-challenged woman from Toby's Tavern, the same one who was at the bird farm that morning. She cleaned herself up from this morning's adventure. Her shoulder-length, copper-blond hair was shinny clean, and the loose curls looked invitingly soft. She had on a long green skirt, sandals, and some kind of blue-green softly draped top. Soft was his overall impression, until she looked up at him. She obviously recognized him. Her green eyes were hard as emerald chips and sparkled with anticipated combat. Damn, she was disturbingly attractive this afternoon. He must be hungry. She was *so* not his type.

The verbal banter was short. They both appeared to be distracted. He really didn't have time to think about this woman and dismissed her from his thoughts as soon as she left the store. He completed his shopping, acquiring all the items on his list and a few extras. He decided to add a big bag of birdseed. There was a large male pheasant hanging around the beach house. Poor guy. If he was an escapee from the old bird farm, Peter figured the bird was as hungry as he was.

CHAPTER 4

THE REALTOR WAS SLEAZY. If Kat weren't so set on this plan, Peter would have approached the purchase in an entirely different manner. He promised to meet with the representative of Lifestyles Realty because they were the listing agency and had originally shown his sister the property. They also allowed him to view the property without interference this morning. Kat wanted to meet the realtor at his office, but Peter talked her out of it. He promised a joint meeting on Wednesday after he had a chance to review the details.

"We are selling more than a property here. It's a whole package. I don't have to tell you all the potential this place has." The realtor, Thomas Bohan, winked at Peter as if to include him in some kind of exclusive businessmen's fraternity. "The island is growing by leaps and bounds," he continued. "This would be a very timely acquisition."

Timely. The word triggered the picture of a small, soft woman with green eyes. Peter never allowed his mind to wander when he was engaged in business of any kind. What was happening here? He wasn't hungry anymore; he fixed lunch and wolfed it down after unloading and stashing the groceries. He needed to stay alert here.

"Of course, timing is important, and I must, in all honesty, tell you that we have another party interested in the property."

Timing. Peter was off into another fantasy. What the hell was wrong with him? It hadn't been that long since he'd had sex, and this self-proclaimed time-challenged woman was so *not* his style. Peter rose abruptly. He grabbed the paperwork, cutting the realtor off mid-spiel.

"OK, let me review this. I'll get back to you."

On Friday afternoon the bakery was packed. I was up to my ears in orders, and there was a line outside on the porch that stretched all the way to Tacoma. I thought Tina would never get back from driving Sadie home. I looked up from ladling out bowls of homemade clam chowder and tomato basil soup and saw Tina's reassuring bulk at the front register. With a sigh, I resumed filling the backed-up orders for to-go specials. Tina slowly and efficiently cleared tables, took in money, and bagged and delivered to-go lunches to those waiting on the porch. She also distributed menus to those electing to wait for a table.

"I'm going to drop this lunch thing. It's just too much work," I muttered.

"You say that every Friday."

The next hour, things settled into a steadier pace.

"I need a bathroom break. Everybody's served except number four. They just sat down," Tina said, heading for the back of the kitchen and our tiny staff-only facilities.

"OK, go." I was momentarily caught up on orders and went out in front, intending to take the order from table four. My timing could not have been worse. My bête noir was sitting with the small, spiky-haired woman from last weekend and another large male. No way was I going to take their order. They would just have to wait for Tina. I checked in with the other tables, trying to keep my back to table four.

"Not much of a selection here," Peter grumbled. He really didn't want Kat to be involved with the real estate agent who sat on his left. She was way too emotional about the old bird farm property.

"The view is fantastic," Kat responded, looking out the window to the bay.

"Yeah, and the food's good too, large portions." Thomas Bohan looked like he lived on large portions. There was something about this man that bothered Peter. If Peter had been a dog, his fur would have stood up every time he was around the man.

"So are you ready to make an offer? I'm telling you this one is time limited. If I weren't so invested in the area already, I would bid on it myself..."

Peter filtered out the man's continuous sales pitch and looked around the room. His eyes settled on the shape of the waitress as she moved back toward the kitchen without stopping to take their order. No, it couldn't be. Peter recognized that shape; it was the Toby's Tavern woman, the same woman that he kept running into and literally ran into at the Prairie Mart. Coupeville was a small town, but this was ridiculous.

I was grateful to see Tina at the register as I moved quickly back toward the kitchen.

"Table four is ready to order," I told her.

"Yeah, so why didn't you take it?" she replied crossly.

Tina usually didn't have an attitude, and I might have thought about the reason for her tone if I wasn't so anxious about seeing that man again. Why was he invading my world? And according to the conversation I overheard, he might be planning to buy the old bird farm. So what? It didn't mean anything to me. So my track record with this man was not exactly stellar. So what? The guy obviously already had a girlfriend. Tina was right; of course I should have taken the order, but I had visions of inadvertently dumping hot soup right in the guy's lap. *Lap, oh no, don't even go there,* I silently scolded myself.

"I can't stand that realtor guy. You know, the one that was at table four," Tina said as we were finishing up the dishes and cleaning out the bakery case.

"Really? Why?" I asked.

"He bought the old church property in front of Mr. Mallory's cabin last year, and then he tried to get Mr. Mallory to sell his place. Bugged the poor man near to death. Then his cat died, and Mr. Mallory swears that the man put a curse on his cat. Wasn't nothing wrong with that cat." Suddenly, Tina went pale and bolted for the bathroom.

"Are you OK?"

"Yeah, some kind of a bug, or maybe it's just this damn menopause thing."

"Do you want me to drop off the leftovers?"

"Nah, I'll have Richard do it."

Richard was Tina's husband. He worked part time at the recycle center/dump and helped us unload the bakery supply truck on Mondays.

I finished shutting down the bakery for the weekend, trying not to think about whatever his name was. Peter, that was it. The timing was so wrong for me to be interested in a man. I needed to find another job. Besides, he had a girlfriend. Not to mention the fact that every time we met, I made a total and complete fool of myself.

CHAPTER 5

"YEAH, JOSH HERE."

Peter was not expecting Josh to answer his call. He usually left a message or got through to Dominic. Josh owned the security company that Peter used for his business. Dominic, Josh's son, was in the Harvard MBA program with Peter, and he was usually the contact person for the security company. Josh was somewhat intimidating to most people. He was somewhere close to sixty, although he was in such good shape that he could easily pass as younger. With two failed marriages and one successful son, he had somewhat of a cloudy past. It was a fact that he was a special operations commander during the Vietnam War. After that, he worked on and off for the government, possibly the CIA, or maybe the FBI or NIS. No one seemed to know for sure, and when you were face to face with Josh, it seemed inadvisable to ask. For the past seven years, he operated his own security company. Dominic had also been military intelligence before he decided to focus on business. After earning his MBA, he joined his father's firm. He described his father as "formidable." The word might have come from his French mother, but it pretty much said it all.

"Dominic is on a case. What do you need?"

That was Josh. Straight to the facts.

Peter asked him to check out Lifestyles Realty and the woman Kat wanted to go into the dog-breeding business with, Marla Rhodes.

"Got it," said Josh, and the line went dead.

Josh was not into social pleasantries.

Good thing I put that annoying male out of my mind because, as it turned out, I had other things to deal with. Turning into my small driveway, I had to slam on the breaks to avoid running into a large, old silver Mercedes. As I opened my car door, Molly, my mother's very wet Portuguese water spaniel, enthusiastically greeted me.

My mother, Tasha, was a very attractive fifty-something-year-old who looked like she was forty-something. I loved my mother, and we had a good relationship, but I did not want to live with her on a permanent basis. When I decided to leave my job at the university, we agreed on a trade. My mother took over my apartment in the University District of Seattle. So here I was, living on the beach in my mother's house, working two jobs to pay my bills, and just trying to find a way through my time-challenged life.

Mom was sitting on the deck with a glass of wine and

a nicely arranged plate of french bread, cheese, and grapes.

"Hello, darling," she said. "Join me? What a fabulous afternoon."

"Hi." My response was a bit less than enthusiastic. I wasn't sure how I felt about Mom dropping back in whenever she felt like it. I poured myself a glass of wine and dropped down into the chair next to her.

"Oh, don't look so down. I promise not to drop in every weekend. This is the first time I've been back for over a month. I just couldn't resist the last weekend in August, and Molly misses the water."

She had a point. She hadn't been back since we made the official house switch.

"How are classes?" I asked. Mom was determined to get her master's degree in psychology and counseling certification in two years.

"Grueling, but I love it."

"You always have been task oriented."

"Wahoo, do I detect a bitter tone here? Where did that come from? Are you angry at me?"

"Oh, Mom. That's not anger. It's jealousy. I have never been able to focus like you can. You always seem to know where you are going and how to get there."

"Not true, my love. I spent years wallowing in indecision before I got up the nerve to leave your father."

Fortunately for both of us, Molly came racing back from the beach. She positioned herself directly between us and shook. The mix of wet sand and dog fur deterred us from finishing that conversation.

"I didn't realize how much Molly was going to miss the beach. With the park so close to the apartment, I thought she would be fine."

"Duh, she is a water dog."

"I may have to leave her with you."

"What? No, you can't," I said, panicked. "I can't keep her. I work two jobs now, and I have to find another one when the nursery closes for the season. My life is crazy."

"Everyone's life is crazy. I am beginning to think that is what life is all about—mostly crazy with short, blessed periods of peace. She won't be any trouble. She's used to it here. There is a dog door, and she can go to the beach whenever she wants. All you have to do is feed her. And speaking of feeding, what do you want for dinner? I brought some fresh halibut."

"Fine."

"Oh, darling, don't pout. You know she won't be any trouble."

"I know. It is just a bad time for me to take on new responsibilities."

"I'll pay for her food, and I'll take her to the groomer once a month."

"OK, you win, as always."

"Oh no, are we back to that again?"

"You have no idea how hard it is to be the child of an overachiever."

Mom went to the kitchen to start dinner while I sat on the deck with Molly and pouted.

The nursery was busy Saturday. Nice weather is not a given on the island, and it brought people out. I was pleasantly exhausted by closing time. Driving down the one-lane road to the beach, I had to admit, if only to myself, that I rather enjoyed my mother's company. She wasn't invading my space and was using the extra bedroom without comment. She made no observations about my housekeeping or lack thereof. She didn't try to use the master bedroom, and she didn't remark on the overgrown flowerbeds or the unwatered lawn. She brought food and she cooked.

Neither she nor Molly was around when I got home, but her bedroom door was closed. There were fresh flowers on the dining room table. About an hour later, they emerged. She fed Molly, and we met on the deck.

"Hi, how was your day?"

"The nursery was really busy. What did you do?"

"There was a negative tide, so Molly and I went clamming, and I did a little weeding. I can't believe I took a nap. I never do that."

Mom steamed the clams and melted butter. I threw a tossed salad together and sliced some french bread.

"I met the people who live on the point. I vaguely remember their parents; do you know them?"

"No."

"She is about your age and has some health issues; I remember that. She does look fragile. Her brother was doing most of the clamming. She is living in the place now, and I understand that he lives in Seattle. She has a Doberman pinscher who Molly adores."

I let my mother's conversation wash over me as I thought about how I was going to convince Mr. Jenson to hire me at the bookstore.

"You know, there is a pheasant living in the hedge row. Poor old guy he must be an escapee from the old bird farm."

"Yeah, I've seen him. I meant to pick up some birdseed for him."

"He would probably appreciate cracked corn more than birdseed. Grammie fed a whole family of them when they first closed down the bird farm."

Mom was gone when I got home Sunday from the nursery. Molly was asleep on the bed in the extra bedroom. She was pitifully happy to see me.

CHAPTER 6

ON MONDAY I PLANNED to sleep late, do laundry, and possibly even weed a flowerbed. If I went for any walks, I was going to stay far away from the bird farm. The phone woke me at 6:00 a.m. It was Tina.

"Richard's sick. Can you meet the truck to unload?"

Tina's husband usually helped unload our weekly supplies for the bakery. I wasn't particularly fond of Tina's significant other, but at her suggestion, I was willing to pay him to help with supplies once a week. It worked out well, and I rarely had to give up my Monday mornings since he started. I didn't even consider calling Sadie. She would have been at the bakery in a heartbeat, unloading that truck by herself.

"I...yeah, I guess. What time does the truck come?"

"About 7:30 a.m. I guess Richard's got the same thing I do. I'm just glad Zach is at my sister's. Couldn't deal with his nonsense on top of this stuff."

"OK, get some rest and let me know how you feel tomorrow."

As I backed out of my driveway, I almost hit a car coming up the beach road. I didn't recognize either the car or the male driver I briefly saw. It looked just a little like…no. It couldn't be, simply not possible.

Tina didn't make it in on Tuesday. On Wednesday, she left early.

"Tina, you have got to see a doctor."

"Yeah," Sadie seconded. "We don't want our customers getting sick."

Sadie wasn't big on sympathy.

I picked Sadie up on Thursday morning as usual. She lived in a small two-story house about a half-mile behind the bird farm. As I drove down the long dirt road leading to her house, I realized that Sadie's property was directly adjacent to the old bird farm. I didn't allow myself to think about why I made that connection. I was definitely not thinking about the man who might be moving in next to my main employer. I simply did not have time in my life for a man—especially that man. Sadie lived with an enormous, old basset hound named Sophie.

Last year, Sadie's daughter sent her a computer. Not only did she learn to use email, but she also discovered Amazon and eBay. To say that she was addicted to online shopping would be disrespectful to my boss, disrespectful but true. She said that if she didn't buy stuff, she would never get any mail, electronic or otherwise. When she first started ordering and receiving, she kept up with the books. She would read what she ordered and give away what she didn't want to keep.

For a while, we had a table of used books for sale by the register at the bakery. Mr. Jenson, who owned the book and antiques store, would come in, buy them all, and resell them at a profit. Then Sadie started selling them to him directly. But lately, I noticed that instead of piles of half-read books stacked all around her house, there were stacks of unopened priority mail and Amazon boxes. Fortunately, Sadie did not watch TV shopping channels.

"Tina still sick?"

"Yes, Richard too and even the dogs. She has a doctor's appointment this morning."

"It's the water."

"What?"

"It's the water that is making them sick. The dogs are the final clue."

"I am still not following you."

"Most of us that live in that area are on community wells. Tina's not. That old farmhouse of hers is on its own well, and I bet they haven't had that water tested since they moved into the place. Community wells have to be tested and treated by law, but if you have an individual well, you are on your own."

"Sadie, that is brilliant. I am going to call Tina as soon as we get to the bakery."

As usual, Sadie baked like a demon all morning and was sagging by lunch. I settled her in with some lunch and some bills at one of the front tables. Tina called to say that she wouldn't be in and that the doctor agreed with Sadie that it could be the water. They couldn't get the water tested right away. In the meantime, they were on antibiotics and using bottled water.

"I am sorry. I know this leaves you in a bind," Tina said.

"No, it's all right. Just get well. I hate to ask this, but do you think you'll make it for the lunch rush tomorrow?"

"Can't promise. Richard is pretty bad, and he likes me around when he's sick."

"Was that Tina?" Sadie asked from the front.

"Yeah. The doctor agreed with you about the well."

"She coming in?"

I didn't want to tell Sadie that Tina wasn't coming in. She would insist on staying.

"I'm staying."

"Sadie, no. I can handle it today, and I will just cancel lunch tomorrow."

Sadie snorted. "I'm staying."

We didn't get a chance to get started on that argument because four people entered the bakery at the same time. The last in line was an absolutely gorgeous Sean Connery type. I sold him the last of the cinnamon rolls.

"Hunk-a hunk-a burning love," Sadie sang from her place at the table as he exited the bakery.

"He was rather fabulous, wasn't he?"

"Back off, kitten. He is too old for you. Leave him for those of us who are experienced."

"Sadie Murphy, you old hussy!"

"Damn right. For him, I might come out of retirement."

Sadie was absolutely exhausted by the time I drove her home. I was very worried about her. I decided to stay long enough to make sure she got some dinner and made it into bed. Sophie, the basset hound, almost tripped us. She was frantic to get out as we were trying to get in.

"Sophie doesn't have a doggie door?" I asked Sadie.

"No, she is a dog school dropout. Never comes when she's called. I tried a door once, but it was when the bird farm was still here, and she would go chase the birds in their pens. Couldn't get her to come home until after dark."

Sadie sank into her favorite chair and nodded off almost instantly. I hadn't realized how bad the house was. Stacks of boxes and unopened mailers were piled everywhere. The stairway to the top floor was completely impassable. The kitchen was a disaster. It took me an hour just to clean it enough to fix Sadie some soup and toast. After she ate, I got her changed and into bed. Amazingly, she did not protest.

"Would you feed Sophie, please?" she asked as she fell asleep again. I fed Sophie and took out three bags of garbage from the kitchen. I promised myself that I would spend all of Monday cleaning Sadie's house and getting her caught up on laundry and grocery shopping. I was ashamed that I hadn't realized what bad shape she was in. I forced the long-term implications of Sadie's situation out of my mind. I simply didn't have time to deal with it right now.

Sadie was still asleep when I stopped to pick her up in the morning. Sophie was asking to go out, but I remembered what Sadie said about her not coming when she was called. I couldn't find a leash, so I used a bathrobe tie and took her out. No amount of encouragement could get her to hurry. I was worried that Sadie would wake up before we got back to the house, but she was still asleep when we retuned. I fed Sophie and left her fresh water. I also left a note for Sadie telling her not to even think about coming into the bakery. I couldn't find her car keys. I wanted to take them with me, but it was getting late.

I was behind before I even started. I put a sign on the door canceling lunch for the day and started on the cinnamon rolls. It was the usual frantic Friday morning, but I was on my own, and by 11:30 a.m., I was frazzled. With my usual poor timing, I decided to stick to the bakery menu for the day—*everything* on the menu. The only concession I made in my solitary state was canceling lunch. I was still baking cookies by lunchtime when Sadie burst in though the back door.

"Why the hell didn't you wake me?" she demanded.

"How did you get here?" I responded.

Fortunately, both answers were put on hold as three customers came in at once. Timing at the bakery was similar to timing in the emergency room at the hospital, according to my friend Shannon. There were times when every exam room was full and the ambulance was on its way, and times when you checked the stock inventory on the crash cart three times. It was all or nothing. Chaos or peace. Sadie automatically took over the baking, saving the last batch of oatmeal raisin cookies from burning and starting on the blackberry cobbler.

I manned—or womaned—the register, which was my least favorite job right behind serving tables. Sadie put the last of the cobbler in the oven. The bakery smelled wonderful. It was 1:00 p.m., and we had almost made it through the day, through the week. We who are time challenged are particularly aware of the time. At 1:01 p.m. Sadie's male hunk from the day before and my male menace walked in together. They sat down at table number four and looked expectantly toward the register.

"We are closed for lunch today," I snapped.

"I thought the bakery was open for lunch on Fridays," the male menace responded.

I really didn't want to have this conversation. "There is a sign on the door."

"No, there isn't."

"Yes, there is!"

I walked out from behind the counter and marched to the front door of the bakery. I was hot and tired, and my timer for the week was running out. I really wanted to grab the sign off the door and slap it down in front of him. It wasn't there. I stepped out on to the porch just in time to see the sign being blown out to sea over the bay. The wind's timing could not have been worse.

"The wind blew it off."

"Uh huh," he responded in a dubious tone. "Well, I think you have a business obligation to fulfill here."

Josh sat quietly, observing with one eyebrow slightly raised. *What is Peter doing antagonizing this cute little girl?* Josh wondered. She was cute, but Josh had given up on the young ones; they were just too much trouble. Of course, he still looked. This wasn't like Peter, though. Despite that fact that he was a brilliant businessman, Peter was basically a caretaker type. It was definitely out of character for him to harass this woman.

Sadie leaned over the counter. "I think we can supply these gentlemen with lunch, Clair."

I couldn't believe it. Sadie was caving. She was taking the side of those men! Just because they looked like male models, just because Sadie thought the hunk-a hunk-a was God's gift to women. I stomped back into the kitchen, throwing my last pathetic verbal volley over my shoulder.

"There will be no selection. You will just have to take what you get."

Josh might not have been interested in pursuing this young woman, but he couldn't pass up that kind of an opening.

"I am sure we will be well satisfied with whatever you can give us," he answered in a velvety smooth voice.

"Isn't she a bit young for you?" Peter asked with an edge in his tone.

"You staking a claim?" Josh asked just to see if he could provoke the younger man.

"Nope, not my type. Go for it, old man. Now, what have you got for me?"

"I am going to ignore that deliberately discriminatory slur regarding my age and sexual prowess. Thomas Bohan, CEO of Lifestyles Realty, moved to the island about two years ago. Had an agency in California prior to that called California Living. No arrests, no warrants, but definitely not on the Better Business Bureau's A list. He has a reputation as a pressure buyer and seller. Nothing proven, but there are all kinds of lingering doubts about unethical conduct—something to do with a federal and state land deals. He was being investigated by the state when he decided to move up here. I'm still digging. Can you go around this clown?"

"No, even if we use another broker, he is still the listing agent, so he is still in the loop."

"I'd have your legal department vet any paperwork, and don't turn your back on this guy."

Sadie placed huge sandwiches made on bakery bread in front of the two men. She winked at Josh. "There is warm blackberry cobbler for dessert too."

"You are a goddess," Josh responded.

The men continued their conversation in low voices as they ate their sandwiches. Sadie was headed toward their table with glasses of iced tea when the front door blew open and the girl with the spiky hair burst in.

"Peter, you rat. You promised I could hear the investigation report. Where's Dominic?"

"Kat, this is Josh…" He was going to say Dominic's father, but he changed it to, "Dominic's boss. Dom is on a case out of the state. Josh, my sister, Katelyn."

"Hi," Kat responded. "Is it OK? Can we buy it? It is just so perfect with most of the outside pens still intact and all the land plus the house and the outbuildings."

"As you can hear, Kat is totally emotionally invested in this property. That is one of the reasons I needed you to look into the seller's agent. Someone here has to be objective."

I overheard the introduction as I walked across the front room to lock the front door, officially closing the bakery for the week. His sister. The woman I thought was his girlfriend was his sister. Why did that make me feel all warm and fuzzy? For some strange reason, I felt so relieved that I even whipped some cream to go on the cobbler and took two servings to the table.

"That looks fabulous," Kat said, reaching over and taking a huge spoonful of her brother's cobbler.

"Hey, wait, that is mine. I ate my entire sandwich so I could have dessert. I was looking forward to it."

"Yes, but I know you'll share it with your sister, Saint Peter." Kat hadn't used her childhood nickname for him in years, and it had probably been years since she was interested in any kind of dessert. How could he resist letting her have it? How could he resist buying the old bird farm for her?

Josh snorted, acknowledging that he heard and filed the nickname.

"Any chance we could get another cobbler here?" Peter called to Clair.

"Possibly, but I might have to charge you double since we are on overtime here."

"Naturally," he muttered.

I went back and started cleaning up the kitchen.

"What's got into you, Clair? You aren't usually this antisocial." Sadie took another helping of cobbler to the table. I went back to loading the dishwasher. Sadie checked them out. She did not charge them double for the third cobbler. And they purchased almost all the remaining items left in the bakery case.

"Clair, do you have the key? Do you want to let these nice people out?"

I dug the keys out of my pocket and tried to hand them to Sadie. She pretended not to see and started counting out the till. With a deep sigh, I went to the front door. The woman was the first out the door and bounded up the steps to the street level. The men followed, both laden with large bakery bags. As they moved out on the porch, the hunk-a hunk-a leaned toward Peter, and I thought that I heard him say, "Oh, by the way, *Saint* Peter, the dog lady's clean."

Not that I was deliberately listening or anything.

CHAPTER 7

SEPTEMBER WAS OFTEN A beautiful month on the island. An Indian summer blessed us, and I enjoyed my tough weekend labors at Rosehip Nursery. On Sunday I took Molly with me. She was still mourning my mother, but she perked up during the car ride. It turned out to be bad timing on my part. I was cleaning up and mulching the last annual bed when I heard the doggie commotion. I looked over to where Molly and the nursery's old golden lab were napping in the sun. They weren't there. I sprinted to the front of the gardens. As I turned the corner to the little garden shed that served as a store, I heard Molly's frantic barking increase to a deafening level. Peter and his sister just got out of the same car I almost backed into coming out of my driveway earlier in the week. A large Doberman pinscher bounded out of the car behind them. Molly was wild with delight, running around the bigger dog in circles, and the nursery's golden lab was keeping up a loud commentary. I had never seen Molly so out of control. She knocked over a large table of fall chrysanthemums and flatly refused to come when I called her.

"Cerberus, sit." The woman gave a quiet command, and the Doberman sat instantly. Molly, with a doggie grin on her saggy face, continued prancing up to the larger dog and racing off to return with her tail wagging and tongue lolling. I tried desperately to catch her as she ran by. The Doberman continued to sit quietly at the woman's side, and I think his eyebrows were just slightly raised. I made a strategically fatal move by chasing Molly. I was so intent on trying to catch my mother's wayward black beast that I ran right into my own bête noir.

Strong male arms closed around my body and saved me from falling face first on the gravel parking lot. He steadied me and looked over my appalling outfit. I had on dirty blue jeans, a dark-orange T-shirt that was probably stained, and a ragged straw hat. "Benjamin Bunny, I presume?"

"Mr. McGregor," I responded, acknowledging our hostile past encounters. By this time, we had a ring of spectators for the circus. Setting me firmly on my feet, Peter casually reached down and caught Molly by the collar. I closed my eyes in total mortification.

"Never chase," he said as he transferred the unrepentant hound's collar to my hand.

"She's not even my dog," I muttered. "I'll just put her in my car until you are finished shopping."

"You don't need to do that." Kat intervened on Molly's behalf. "I think she has calmed down." Molly, who was panting hard, tipped her large black saggy head up at me as if to say, "I'm calm. I'm in control. What is all the fuss about?" I loosened my chokehold on her collar, and she sank into a black puddle at my feet. Kat released the Doberman with a quiet "OK," and the two dogs exchanged doggie greetings. People drifted away since the show was apparently over. The golden lab wandered off in search of a warm patch of sunlight, and Peter righted the knocked over table.

"Oh, you are the lady from the bakery. Hi, I am Katelyn Cameron. Great cinnamon rolls. Do you work here too?"

"Yes," I mumbled and began picking up the scattered pots of mums and replacing them on the table. What I really wanted to do was slink away and lick at my embarrassment in a very quiet place. "Thank you," I managed to choke out as Peter helped replace the flower containers.

"No charge," he said with a smile.

I grabbed Molly and retuned to my abandoned garden bed. Amazingly, she came without protest.

"You are a terrible dog," I told her. "And don't think for a minute that I am not going to tell Mom on you."

She had the nerve to lick my hand. I wasn't really mad at Molly. I was furious at the universe and at my bad timing. Why did I make a fool of myself every time this man was in my vicinity? And of course the worst part was that all indicators pointed to the fact that he now *lived* in my vicinity. Maybe even on my own beach. I couldn't think about that right now. I simply didn't have time. After work I drove home with artichokes for dinner and beautiful, big russet-colored chrysanthemums for the porch. I told Molly that I was never taking her with me to work again. She was sound asleep on the back seat.

CHAPTER 8

ON MONDAY I WAS at Sadie's by nine o'clock in the morning. Not that I had a watch on. Watches didn't work on me. I had been given scores of them over the years, and the batteries gave up immediately when I put them on. Or, for totally inexplicable reasons, they were too fast or too slow or quit altogether as soon as I started wearing them.

I was surprised to see Tina's old pickup truck parked in front of Sadie's garage. I should have known that Tina had been picking up groceries for Sadie. I knocked briefly on the back door and walked into the kitchen. Sophie came to greet me, but discovering that I had no edible offerings, she shuffled back into the living room. Sadie was in her favorite chair, and Tina was standing beside her, armed with a vacuum cleaner.

"I cannot clean this carpet with these boxes piled all over the place," said Tina.

"Well, no one asked you to," Sadie responded in a decidedly cranky tone.

"Hi, guys. What's up?" I decided it was time to enter the fray.

"What is this, a gathering of the coven?" Sadie said, acknowledging my presence.

"Tell her we've got to get rid of some of these boxes," Tina ordered me. "You can hardly move around in here. Talk some sense into her."

"This is my house, and these are my boxes. I don't want them moved, and I don't care if the carpet is vacuumed or not."

I knew that my timing was probably wrong, but I had to stage some kind of intervention.

"These boxes are so hard to open. How about I fight with the cardboard, and you decide what you want done with the contents?"

No response from Sadie.

"Do you have a pair of heavy scissors?"

"Kitchen," Sadie grumbled, which I took as reluctant agreement.

"Tina, will you help me find them?"

Tina found the scissors under a pile of old newspapers and unopened mail on the kitchen table.

"I swear I had this kitchen table cleared when I was here Thursday," I said.

"Some of these are bills, and I bet they are overdue. I don't think Sadie's been paying them," Tina said, sorting through the pile. "Clair, what are we going to do? I've been picking up groceries, and sometimes she will let me do a load of laundry, but she needs more than that. Every ounce of energy she has goes into the bakery."

"I know, but she loves it so much. I took me months to get her to agree to work half days."

"Love it or not, something has to be done on the home front. Do you think we should call her daughter?" Sadie's daughter lived in Philadelphia. She emailed weekly but visited only once a year.

We didn't make much progress on the pile of boxes. Sadie had trouble deciding what to do with the contents once they were opened. We did get some scrambled eggs, toast, and tea into her, but only because we agreed to join her.

Sadie hated having her space invaded. I could tell that she both appreciated and loathed what Tina and I were doing. We had to shift the focus before she totally rebelled.

"Tina, what have they found out about your water?" I asked.

"It is definitely contaminated. They have to do more tests to find out what it is, and it's damn expensive. We are still using bottled water for drinking and cooking, and I am washing our clothes at the laundromat in town."

I had a timely idea, which was rare for me.

"I bet Sadie would let you wash your clothes here."

"Sure, and you can fill plastic jugs with drinking water from my tap too," Sadie replied.

"That would be great, thanks, Sadie." Tina raised her eyebrows at me as if to say "good one, Clair!"

"Do you have any idea where the contamination is coming from?" I asked, still trying to keep the focus off Sadie.

"That's the worst part. It could be that the septic tank is

seeping into the well."

"Does that mean a new septic tank?"

"And a new well," Tina responded dejectedly.

She had one daughter who was recently married and worked as a nurse's aide at the hospital. One son was in the army, and another still lived at home. There was no money in the family for these kinds of major projects.

"You could try shocking the well and see if it holds," Sadie said.

"What does that mean?" I asked.

"You add a bunch of chemicals, mostly chlorine, and then you test again in a few weeks. If the contamination is from the septic tank, the shocking won't help, but if it is some kind of external contamination, shocking should take care of it."

"Sadie, how do you know so much about wells?" I asked, truly impressed.

"I was president of the water board several years ago."

With Sadie's spirit restored, we were able to accomplish much more. We changed her bed and got the laundry caught up. The worst part was that we didn't get much floor space cleared. She was stubbornly resistant to going through the boxes. The best part was that Tina was able to set up a time to come in twice a week to do laundry and pick up water. This was going to work out well. It gave Sadie some of the help she needed but would refuse if it were offered outright. It gave Tina free laundry and water, and it gave us both a chance to keep a closer eye on Sadie's home life. The timing gods were smiling on us.

The two weeks that Peter allotted for himself to be away from the office were almost over. He would return to Seattle on Monday. He worked up an offer on the bird farm after thoroughly reviewing property values on the island. He would take the offer to his lawyer to have it checked out before he presented it to the real estate agent, and he would insist on using his own broker for the deal. Kat was over the moon. Peter still wasn't convinced that a dog-breeding business was a good idea for her. It was doubtful whether the endeavor could financially break even.

On the upside, the land was probably a good investment. He admitted to himself that his agreement to buy was being made partly on an emotional basis. Kat needed something to do with her life that brought her joy. He had been watching over his sister since he was a teenager. She was an unexpected child of his older parents, and they encouraged a caretaking role for him since her birth. He did admit that the old bird farm property was the perfect venue for the dog-breeding scheme. But it would need a rather substantial infusion of capital to be operational. The outdoor pens would need studier fencing for the dogs. The outbuildings all needed work, and the house needed updating. He would have to find a good contractor, and then it would be necessary for him to make frequent weekend inspection tours. The thought of frequent visits to the island made him feel happy for some reason. It shouldn't have; it was a hassle to catch the ferry on the weekends, and it took way too much time to drive around the Deception Pass Bridge route. He thought back to Clair's soft, shapely body pressed close to him as kept her from falling at the nursery. Oh no, he did not need another rescue project. Still, all his memories of that woman brought a smile to his face.

"Peter, can't you stay just one more day? Marla just called, and she can make it down tomorrow. She hasn't seen the property yet, and I want you to meet her."

Marla Rhodes, or the dog lady, as Josh referred to her, was Kat's prospective partner in this doggie endeavor. Josh said she was clean, but Peter was still concerned about her taking advantage of his very vulnerable sister.

"OK, one more day, but that has to be it, Kat. I've already taken off far more time than I should have."

"Nonsense, you rarely take time off. And besides, you are in constant communication with the office, even from here. You know, Peter, all work and no play—"

"Yeah, yeah, yeah. Come on. Let's make tuna sandwiches for lunch. Do we have any bakery bread left?"

CHAPTER 9

ON MONDAY NIGHT AT 1:30 a.m., I still couldn't sleep. We who are time challenged often have trouble sleeping. It has something to do with timing, I'm sure.

"OK, I give up. I'm up, I'm up," I said, sitting up on my side of the bed. Molly rose from her own bed and came over to thrust her cold, wet nose into my hand. She would not sleep on my bed as she did with Mom, but at least she moved into my room and accepted a huge L.L. Bean dog bed purchased and delivered thanks to Mom's Visa. I mentioned in a phone conversation with her that Molly was still sleeping on the bed in the guest bedroom.

We went out into the living room, which was lit by an amazing harvest moon shining in through the floor-to-ceiling windows. I tried reading in bed. I tried sleepy time tea. I tried eating every carbohydrate in the house and watching mind-numbing TV reruns. I tried slow, deep counting while concentrating on my breathing. Nothing worked. Sleep was in another time zone. The moon whispered that a walk by the water might be the answer.

I found a large magenta-and-gold Huskies sweatshirt, probably left over from my brother's brief college encounter. I pulled it on over my lime-green satin pajamas. The beautiful orange moon hung low over the water and filled the yard with a misty light.

I stepped into a pair of Mom's leather clogs on the porch. The clogs were about two sizes too big for me, and I had a hard time getting over the logs to the hard, packed sand on the beach. Molly wasn't helping. She was thrilled with a post-midnight beach walk and ran around me in circles. If I hadn't been having so much trouble just walking, I would have noticed the beach fire before I reached the beach. Who has a beach fire at two o'clock in the morning? Without conscious thought, I moved toward it.

Peter watched her approach his fire. The big male Doberman let out a single bark by way of a welcome as they came into the circle of light.

"Great outfit," he remarked in a casual tone.

"Oh, you are just jealous," I replied without rancor. Something about the middle-of-the-night meeting on a fire-lit beach freed me to respond naturally to my adversary.

"Quite right," he responded. "I don't think I could ever put together such a getup. Want a marshmallow?"

I didn't ask why he was roasting marshmallows on the beach at two o'clock in the morning, and he didn't ask what was keeping me awake at the same hour. We sat, taking turns roasting marshmallows on a long stick. I leaned back against a log, listening to the crackling fire, the lapping of the water at the tide's edge, and the soft sounds of the dozing dogs.

"Beautiful Doberman. He seems so gentle."

"He is. He belongs to my sister. His name is Cerberus."

"As in the dog that guards the gates of hell?"

"Top marks! Five years ago, Kat was diagnosed with lupus. She was a fragile kid and sick on and off all her teen years, but this definitive diagnosis was unexpected. She was in and out of the hospital for over six months. She was so depressed that I wasn't sure she would recover. When she left the hospital, she had to have a lot of help. One of her caretakers brought in a Doberman pincher puppy. Kat says he brought her back from the gates of hell."

Silence stretched out between us. I looked up at the sky.

"We used to spend the summers up here. My brother and I would sleep out on the beach. August was always my favorite month because there were always so many shooting stars. So many chances to wish…"

Her wistful tone made Peter want to put his arms around her and ask why the chances were all in the past, but he thought he might frighten her, so he stayed where he was and studied the night sky. She was quiet for so long that he thought she might have fallen asleep. The fire was dying down, and a fine mist was starting to settle. Clair pushed herself up to her knees and then to her feet. She picked up the clogs she had discarded earlier and started to walk away.

"Thanks for the marshmallows," I threw over my shoulder.

"Hey, what are neighbors for?"

Peter watched her walk down the beach and into the

dark, Molly trailing close behind. He stayed in the faint circle of firelight. He searched the dark, starlit sky. It seemed that he was always searching since his parents died. He was so sure of himself before his parents' death. So sure of who he was and where he was going. He successfully took over his father's company, diversified and expanded it. He managed the trust they set up for Kat and made a profit on investing some of the capital. He did his best to support his sister, so why did his life suddenly seem rather empty?

Sleep, he just needed some sleep. Tomorrow he would be back in the city. Tomorrow he would be busy at work. Tomorrow he would be fine.

"Come on, Cerberus. Let's put out his fire and turn in, buddy."

CHAPTER 10

SEPTEMBER WAS SLIPPING AWAY. I worked to harvest the apples at the nursery, and by the end of the month, that job would be over for the year. I was no closer to finding another. I approached Mr. Jenson about working weekends in his store and helping him build up his book search business, but he hadn't given me a reply yet. Sadie perked up since Tina was coming to her house twice a week. But that would be coming to an end soon. Inexplicably, an animal carcass was found floating in the well. They shocked the well, as Sadie suggested, and the subsequent testing indicated that the water was safe to use again. The question of how the well got contaminated was still unanswered. The health department said that it was probably fairly recent because of the resulting sickness. If the source of the contamination occurred long before, the family would have either shown signs before now or built up immunity to the bacteria. Tina said that she was just grateful that the whole thing was over and that they didn't need to drill a new well or replace the septic system.

On Wednesday afternoon, Tina and I were finishing up at the bakery. The place smelled like the apple cake and the almond sugar cookies in the shape of leaves and squirrels we were featuring this week. Business was slow that afternoon, so we decided to make ourselves a pot of tea. We settled at table number four because it had the best view of the bay, but we weren't looking at the water. This was a serious strategy session. Tina had been bringing out Sadie's mail once a week, and we were dealing with it. I started including her personal bills with prewritten checks for her to sign when I presented her the bakery bills every Thursday. Sadie was too sharp not to notice that there were two piles of bills each week paid out of two different accounts. She hadn't said a word about it. It was a silent acknowledgement of her need for help. But what were we going to do when Tina no longer had a reason to go to Sadie's house twice a week?

"She flat out refuses to get someone to come in and clean," I said.

"I know. I've had that same discussion with her," Tina replied.

"Tina, can you keep going in at least weekly and do enough to get her by? We might be able to talk her into hiring you. I'll tell her that you need the money."

"Well, that wouldn't be a lie. I could do it on Mondays after Richard and I unload the truck."

"Did you ever get ahold of her daughter?"

"Didn't I tell you? She says she's been trying for years to get Sadie to move to Philadelphia. Sadie refuses to leave the island, and she also flat out refuses any suggestions her daughter makes about help."

We couldn't think of any other timely interventions, so we sorted Sadie's mail.

"Hey, this is the same letter we got," Tina burst out.

"What letter?"

"I thought it was just an ad or one of those nonprofit letters asking for donations, so I opened it. But it's the same letter we got about two weeks ago. It says that someone wants to buy our house and that they will give us a good price for it. It came just when we thought we might have to put in a new well and septic tank. That's why I remember it. I think I still have it. Sadie's letter says the same thing. And it's not signed, just like ours. Just some instructions to reply to this post office box."

"Well, I am sure that Sadie's not interested in selling, but put it in her pile to review. Sounds like someone is trying to buy up property in the area."

The door to the bakery opened and two people came in. Three more followed them shortly after that, and our tea break was over.

Their bid on the bird farm was accepted, and Peter was going up to the island for the weekend to sign the papers and meet with his sister and Marla. They needed to plan an ongoing strategy for the renovations. He had his legal department outline the major points of a business plan and merger between Kat and Marla. It was going to be complicated because the land would remain in Kat's trust, and the breeding dogs belonged to Marla. Peter admitted that Marla had all the knowledge and expertise needed to run the operation, and as far as he could determine, she wasn't trying to take advantage of his sister. All the business suggestions came originally from Kat. He still had to find a contractor for the renovation work on the property.

He was finishing up the week's projects and wondering how he could maneuver another meeting with Clair when his office door burst open. He looked up at the very beautiful and agitated woman moving determinedly toward his desk.

"Apparently, I have to actually brave you in your den to get you to respond. You are always unavailable when I call, and you haven't answered any of my messages."

Peter rose from his seat as he felt the waves of angry tension coming from the tall, slender blonde in front of his desk.

"Cynthia, I apologize. I'm still catching up from the time I took off in August, and every extra minute has gone into this land acquisition and business merger I'm working on for my sister."

"Yes, I know that you actively manage your sister's trust. Do you take a management fee? You probably should make it variable so it can be increased when you spend more time and resources on it." She leaned slightly over the desk.

Peter did not want to discuss his sister or her trust with Cynthia. Suddenly, he didn't want to discuss anything with this woman. They had been together on and off for about a year. She was a relationship banker at one of the banks his corporation used. There was no question that she was his preferred type. She was sharp and focused, and she had a beautiful body. Their usual pattern was to go out once a week and sleep together. They were also perfect partners for any social obligation in either of their business worlds, and they ran in the same social circles. He deliberately let the silence grow between them.

"Peter, what is wrong with you? You seem so distracted." The woman who stood before his desk was almost vibrating as she spoke. He knew that Cynthia was high energy, which usually appealed to him. But right now, he was pleased that his desk was between them, and he made no move to walk around it.

"Sorry. I have to go up to the island tonight to finalize the land deal."

"What?" she virtually screeched at him. Peter wondered if her voice had always been so unpleasant. As if finally realizing his strange mood, she made a visible effort to relax her body as she moved around the desk toward him. "Well, I know you'll do what you told me you would. What time will you pick me up tomorrow night?"

"What?"

"The symphony gala tomorrow night. What time will you pick me up?"

"Oh, Cynthia. I'm sorry. I completely forgot about it."

She closed the distance between them and was now standing directly in front of him. Peter instinctively moved out from behind the desk. She possessively threw an arm around his neck.

"You forgot? Darling, the bank is sponsoring this event. We talked about it months ago. It is not like you to forget."

"Cynthia, I really am sorry, but there is no way I can make it back in time for the gala tomorrow night." He removed her arm from around his neck. He may have been slightly concerned that she would strangle him.

He felt shards of ice shooting at him from her light-blue eyes.

"You could have at least had the decency to tell me earlier in the week." She snapped her jaw together, obviously holding back the remaining words that wanted to jump out and assault him. He could almost taste the words she wanted to hurl at him: jerk, ass, and ratfink—well, probably not ratfink, that wasn't her style. He deserved the words. *How long have I unconsciously wanted to break up with this woman?* he wondered. He watched her move her beautiful body carefully and quickly across his office, and he braced himself for the slamming door. When it came, he felt a great release, as though he just escaped in a very timely manner.

The meeting with Thomas Bohan went off without a hitch. Of course, the man whined about Peter choosing to use his own broker and the fact that his offer, which was $10,000 under the asking price, had been accepted. Peter let the man's unpleasant voice drone on. Kat's joy over the purchase was well worth putting up with the bore. The closing was set for next month in Seattle. The agent agreed to allow them access to the property for the weekend to plan the renovations needed. He turned the keys over to Peter with a spiel about a contractor that he would recommend for the job.

Marla was waiting for them at the bird farm. They started with the outside spaces because it looked like it was going to rain. They all agreed on replacing the bird netting with metal fencing. There were fifty large bird pens, about 25 × 20 feet, enclosed with bird netting on the sides and top. Open, grassy pathways snaked between the pens. There was a large, open field beyond those, with better fencing, that circled the exterior of the property, except for two outbuildings and the house with the lawn in front of it. Marla wanted at least twenty of the enclosures to have closed shelters built. This would house at least twenty dogs with indoor and outdoor access. The long one-story cement outbuilding had basic electricity and one bathroom, but it was in terrible shape. It would probably need to be gutted and completely redone. Still, the structure was sound, and Marla planned on using it for indoor kennels and a grooming area.

Peter suggested using the second outbuilding for an office, but the girls had already decided that, with some work, it would make a perfect nursery for expectant and nursing mother dogs. Both buildings would need some kind of heating system, which meant that the office would have to be in the house. Peter unlocked the door just as the heavy mist turned into a steady downpour. The girls, as Peter thought of them, had apparently already discussed the house as well. They planned to use the living or dining room for the office. The kitchen and bathroom on the first level needed some updating and the carpets throughout needed to be replaced with something dog friendly. Marla planned to move in upstairs and live in the master bedroom. That left two extra bedrooms free for unplanned, future use.

The girls looked at the space and discussed flooring possibilities. Peter looked at the window frames and the heating unit and noted that the roof apparently did not leak. On Saturday afternoon, nothing was open in Coupeville for lunch. They would have to drive somewhere because Peter was hungry, and having spent the night at the beach house, he knew there was nothing there to fix for lunch. His sister's lifestyle was a constant mystery and worry to her brother. They decided to drive down to the island to get lunch. Marla declined their invitation to join, saying that she had to head back to the peninsula because she was unable to find anyone to come in and care for her dogs overnight.

The rain let up slightly for their thirty-minute drive down the island. The weather was not conducive to a walk on the beach after lunch, so Peter was struggling to come up with a way to accidentally spend some time with Clair. He would have to stock the beach house up on food. Maybe if he shopped at the Prairie Center Mart, he would run into her again.

CHAPTER 11

MOLLY AND I WERE mopping. It was too wet to work at the nursery, not that there was much left to do there anyway. My mother offered me a weekend at the apartment, but I declined. I knew she would want to take me shopping or out to lunch or dinner or both.

"Molly, your roommate is an idiot. I could have gone to a museum. I could have had Indian or Chinese for dinner. I forgot how dreary this place is when the weather changes," I said.

I called Sadie to see if she needed anything. She said no and that she and Sophie were going to take a nap. I put on loud Celtic music. I did laundry and cleaned the bathrooms. In the middle of cleaning out the refrigerator, I decided I couldn't take it anymore.

"Molly, I have to get out of here for a while." The rain was on hold temporarily, so I decided that this was a good time to pick up some firewood. Fires were good. They warmed up the house both physically and emotionally. I could have had it delivered but that cost extra. I figured I could load it in my trunk, put down a tarp, and get the rest in the back seat and on the floor. My plan after that was to splurge on a video rental and pick up a takeout pizza for a fun-filled evening. It wasn't a great plan, but it beat cleaning out the refrigerator and watching the rain with a Portuguese water dog. I had to save something to do on Sunday. I left Molly at home, protesting. I couldn't fit much wood in the car if Molly came.

The berry farm on the west beach road sold wood in the fall and winter. I got slightly drenched while loading about a quarter of a cord into my car. Luckily, I had on my black rain boots with pink flamingos and my yellow rain slicker—both were treasures I found at the Goodwill when I lived in the University District. The temperature dropped, and the wind picked up. I was grubby and dripping when I walked in to order my pizza. Coupeville recently acquired a pizza parlor. Pizza Plus was doing very well and strategically positioned itself next to the one video rental in town. So here was the deal: you placed your order at the pizza place, and while they made your pizza, you ran next door and rented a video. I knew this because I had checked both places for a possible weekend jobs. The island teenagers had gotten there first. Oh well, I might have also been just a tad overqualified. As my mother liked to remind me, I graduated cum laude from the University of Washington with a major in English literature, which pretty much qualified me for nothing. My previous job as a research assistant in the history department did give me some good credentials, and I knew I should build on that. I probably shouldn't have quit that job, but it really wasn't what I wanted to do when I grew up.

Sometimes I wondered when I was going to grow up, but not tonight. Tonight I was on a mission to find the perfect video. The adolescent store clerk informed me that anything that wasn't "new" or "newer" was two for the price of one. Boy was this my lucky night. I stopped briefly at the "new" release shelf, but it was empty. That was probably OK because I wasn't particularly into either sex or violence tonight. I wandered past the "newer" release sections, deciding I'd look there later. I headed for the foreign films section, which consisted of exactly ten DVDs. I snagged one obscure offering and moved over to the family section. It might be a good night for *The NeverEnding Story.*

It is Saturday evening, and there probably won't be any current videos left to rent in the one rental place in Coupeville, Peter thought. Kat was next door ordering pizza. Another of his sister's unexplainable lifestyle choices was that she did not have a satellite dish or any kind of cable connection.

That meant that there was literally nothing on her TV. Of course, there was nothing on satellite TV either, but there was at least a whole lot more of nothing. Peter picked up a historical DVD about Beatrix Potter; Kat would like it. It reminded him of Clair in her Benjamin Bunny mode. He still hadn't come up with an idea of how to see her this weekend. He decided that he should also pick up an action/drama and maybe a comedy to get him through the night. He headed for the comedy section.

⁓

The candy selection was right in front of the checkout counter. It caught my attention. It shouldn't have; after all, I'd already ordered a pizza and probably had a bag of microwave popcorn in the back of one of my kitchen cabinets. I decided to grab a bag of licorice sticks and maybe a Mounds or Snickers bar. While I was deciding between the two candy bars, I realized that I also needed to include a comedy selection in my menu of entertainment for the evening. After all, these were two-day rentals, and I still had Sunday to get through. The weather report said rain all weekend. I hadn't actually checked the weather report, but it always said there was a "possibility of rain." Balancing the two DVDs I already chose, a bag of microwave popcorn in case I didn't have one at home, a bonus bag of black licorice sticks, and two candy bars, I turned the corner into the comedy aisle.

"Oh no." A moan slipped from me involuntarily. It seemed that the timing gods had already set up a cosmic comedy. Peter stood in the exact center of the small comedy section, looking like a magazine picture entitled "Country Gentleman Selects Evening Entertainment." I was suddenly totally aware of all the wet-wood dirt clinging to me. The rain had frizzed my hair to unmanageable dimensions, I had on not a lick of makeup, and my rain boots were leaving muddy tracks on the floor. In contrast, the rain made Peter's hair look like silk. I wanted to touch it in the worst way. I thought if I opened my rain slicker it might help my appearance a little, but that caused all the items I'd carefully balanced to shift and cascade to the floor, right at Peter's feet. Why was I so cursed with such bad timing? The universe was mute in answer, as usual.

Peter saw her the moment she turned into the comedy section. She had on another unbelievably outrageous outfit: a large, yellow sou'wester-type rain jacket, some kind of green-and-orange sweater under that, and a pair of black jeans stuffed into a pair of shiny black rain boots with bright-pink flamingos all over them. Her hair was a glorious riot framing her face in an almost halo. Her cheeks were pink from the cold and her eyes sparkled. Peter couldn't believe that his timing was so great. He'd been trying for days to come up with a way to meet this woman again, and here she was, delivered to him right in the middle of the video rental store. He blessed the universe and bent down to help her retrieve her loot.

"Settling in for hibernation?" he asked, looking over her stash of DVDs and candy.

"Exactly, and you? Somehow you don't strike me as the Beatrix Potter type."

"I have depths that might amaze you."

"No doubt."

"Actually, the Beatrix Potter DVD is for my sister."

"Well, that's comforting to know."

"I could comment on your choice of viewing material

if I was feeling rude."

"Oh, go for it!" Why did I always get adversarial with this man? Well, not always. The post-midnight scene on the beach flashed into my mind. We were actually gentle with each other the last time we met. But that was then, and now I looked like a horror movie reject, and he was considering an attack on my personal movie selections. Suddenly, I was reconsidering my decision to forgo videos with violence in them.

"No, the better part of valor advises me to withhold comment."

"Very honorable. No doubt one of those hidden parts of your personality."

"Precisely, may I help you—?"

Peter found himself momentarily without words. What he really wanted to say was, "May I kiss you?," "May I take you to bed?," or any number of equally unacceptable propositions. His brain had, uncharacteristically, switched to the stupid channel. Fortunately for his ego, she cut him off.

"I doubt we have the same taste…in anything."

"Hey, that's not true. I love your cinnamon rolls." Peter groaned when he heard the words coming out of his mouth. He loved her cinnamon rolls. Very classy. That would make any woman want to jump right into bed with him. What was wrong with him? He didn't have trouble with women. He had to switch off the stupid channel.

"Well…good." I simply couldn't think of a snappy comeback. I wasn't really listening to his words anyway. I was watching his mouth, looking at the shape of his lips, and wondering how they would fit on top of mine. And wondering how it would feel if he moved those beautifully sculptured lips down…

Suddenly, I was really glad that I had opted out of picking any movies displaying overt sex. It wasn't that I objected to sex. It was just that it was unavailable to me at this time, and I didn't need to increase my lusting quota . The man in front of me already amped that quota way up over my tolerance level, and he wasn't even touching me. I grabbed *The Gods Must Be Crazy* and started to turn back toward the checkout counter.

"Hey, I was going to pick that one." Peter was a desperate man. The universe had delivered this woman right to him, and now she was getting away. Could he be losing his timing?

"It's not exactly a recent release."

"I like vintage humor."

I started walking toward the checkout counter at a smart pace. He was right behind me.

I then dumped the DVDs, popcorn, licorice, and both candy bars on top of the wood piled in the passenger seat. I hoped that my pizza was ready because I needed to get out of Dodge or, more specifically, Coupeville. I was planning on an evening of self-pity and pizza.

Oh no. My timing was bad, but this was beyond bad. I couldn't find a parking place close to the building, and I had to walk for miles. Peter was standing near the door to the pizza place with his sister. She saw me enter the crowded restaurant and turned toward me with a smile.

"Oh, Clair, hi. I guess we all had the same idea. Peter

said he saw you next door."

The place was busy and crowed. Well, a comparatively small number constituted a crowd in Coupeville. There were four other people waiting for orders besides Peter, his sister, and me. Kat moved to stand between Peter and me. She continued in her soft, breathless voice.

"I am not much of a cook. Poor Peter, he's half-starved when he stays with me."

I looked over at the object of her concern. "He doesn't appear to be wasting away."

Peter jumped into the conversation

"I'd take that as a compliment, but I am sure that is not the spirit in which it was intended."

Kat raised her eyebrows. She could feel the tension between these two. It wasn't a negative tension, but there was definitely something there. Interesting.

My number was finally called. I rushed up to pay for my pizza. Peter's number was called next, and he moved up behind me. I grabbed my box and broke for the door. Kat stopped me with a gentle hand on my arm.

"Clair, why don't you join us tonight? We can pig out and watch movies together. It'll be fun."

I was terrible at saying no. I always had to practice if I was going to turn someone down. Kat watched me search for an excuse.

"Please come. It gets so lonely on the beach this time of year."

"I…Molly."

Kat didn't know exactly what was going on between this

woman and her brother, but she was determined to provide the opportunity they both seemed to need.

"Oh, bring Molly with you. Cerberus loves her." She saw her brother moving toward them with two large boxes of pizza, and she didn't want to give Clair another opportunity to say no.

"Great, then we will see you in about half an hour."

No. No. No. How did I let her talk me into sharing the evening with them? Earth calling Clair, because you really want to go, I admonished myself. I made the drive to the beach in record time and jumped into the shower. I needed to look good tonight in the worst way. Deep in the recesses of my closet was a dark-brown velour set that Mom bought me last fall. Velour probably wasn't fashionable anywhere else in the world anymore, but before and after the teenage years, no one cared about fashion on the island. Comfort and warmth were the motivators for clothing purchases here. When she gave it to me, I was certain that I would never have occasion to wear it. But my mother was a Libra, and her sense of style was flawless, so I kept it just in case. Mom said I looked fabulous in it, and I wanted to look fabulous tonight. I stashed the pizza in the oven to keep it warm, fed Molly, put on some mascara, and blow-dried my hair. I thought about putting on more makeup, but I didn't want to look like I was trying too hard. I had to admit that the color of the outfit was perfect; it brought out all the red highlights in my hair and the green of my eyes.

"I invited Clair to come down and share pizza and DVDs with us." Kat said softly on the drive back to the beach. Peter almost ran off the road. "I hope that is all right," she added, suddenly afraid that she might have misinterpreted the situation.

"No, that's fine," Peter answered so quickly and with such a positive tone that Kat let out a small laugh. Her brother looked over at her. "I love you, Katelyn Cameron."

Peter was absolutely the best brother any woman could have, but he rarely verbalized his feelings.

Once home, he put the pizza in the oven to keep it warm. Kat fed Cerberus and disappeared into a large storage area near the front door.

"Peter, would you help me with these boxes?" She pointed to several large boxes labeled "Halloween." "Just put them on the loveseat in the living room. I think I will decorate the house tomorrow." That was decidedly out of character for his sister, but he did as she asked without comment.

When Molly and I arrived, Peter was fixing a salad. Cerberus got up to greet Molly, and they both went to lie in front of the fire in the living room. We followed them with our trays of food. Kat took the only single chair. "Sorry about the boxes. They're Halloween decorations."

The boxes were taking up an entire leather love seat. The only other seats available were on a leather couch. Peter set his tray on the big truck that served as a coffee table. "I'm going to get a beer. Anybody else want one?"

"I'll have one." *I need it*, I thought to myself as I eyed the seating arrangements. By the time the first DVD was over, we had devoured most of the pizza.

"Well, I'm for bed. For some reason, I am very sleepy tonight. It must be the change in the weather." Kat came over and dropped a kiss on her brother's forehead on her way out of the room.

Peter got up and put in *The Gods Must Be Crazy.* He added another log to the fire, which meant the dogs had to move out of the way briefly. They seemed to understand the process and resettled themselves without comment. Peter could have moved to the chair his sister had vacated, but he didn't even consider it. Sitting next to Clair without touching her was killing him. She looked fantastic tonight.

All the way though the Beatrice Potter DVD, Peter and I tried hard not to touch each other. It was a big couch, but occasionally our hands brushed as we reached for our food or our beers. If he didn't touch me soon, I was either going to scream or take Molly home and eat all my candy at one time. He brought one hand up and smoothed my hair, following it down to my throat and slipped it behind my neck. Then he brought his mouth down to cover mine. It was a gentle kiss, as if he were trying to match the shape of my lips perfectly with his. His other hand moved up to cup my breast.

CHAPTER 12

TASHA FINISHED HER MORNING prayers and morning exercises. Now, over her second cup of coffee, she could plan her Saturday. She was sorry that Clair chose not to accept her invitation to spend the weekend together. She enjoyed her daughter's company and wished their relationship weren't so strained. Clair resented her on some level. Tasha was not going to push it. When her daughter was ready, she would be there. In the meantime, she would take whatever level of relationship Clair was comfortable with. Tasha tried not to offer too many suggestions; she knew that Clair had to find her own way and in her own time.

So a whole beautiful, misty silver day waited for her. What would she do with it? Of course, there was always reading and studying and writing her thesis, and she would do some of that. But today was a play day. Tasha was just leaning to play again. The fun part of her almost died during her marriage. She was determined to nourish those parts of herself that she stuffed away for so long. She was also working on giving up guilt. She was good at guilt, and it was proving hard to give up. The apartment seemed empty without Molly. It was clean because she allowed herself to hire someone to clean it twice a month. That had been a battle with guilt that she won. If she were being absolutely honest with herself, she worked right alongside the cleaner, fixed her an elaborate lunch, and grossly overpaid the woman. Maybe guilt wasn't banished completely. If Molly were still living with her, they would have gone for a long walk in the park, even in the rain. But Molly was living with Clair. Molly needed the beach, and Clair needed Molly. Tasha needed somewhere to play today.

She read over the "What to Do" section of the *Seattle Times* and decided on visiting the small museum located on the university grounds. She could go to the symphony season opening tonight but decided against that. Her ex-husband would probably be there. He would go only for the gala benefit opening; there would be other weekends for the symphony. She felt no need to either approach or avoid her former husband. The university's music department was offering a small chamber orchestra in concert that night. They were playing Vivaldi, one of her favorite composers; maybe she would go to that. The University District had a wonderful selection of mostly cheap international food offerings. She would also treat herself to dinner, maybe Indian or Chinese.

She walked across the campus to the museum. One of the many great things about her apartment was its proximity to the campus. She blessed her parents again for all they gave her, both tangible and intangible. A cool, gentle mist accompanied her, but she was a Pacific Northwest girl. It was fine. She loved the fall and relished the colors of the changing leaves as she walked the almost-deserted pathways across the university grounds. The interior of the museum was dim and hushed. It seemed almost abandoned. An older docent passed out a written explanation of the major exhibits and gestured discretely toward the donation container. Tasha stuffed ten dollars in the container. The museum was small. Its main emphasis was on Pacific Northwest Indian culture. The main exhibit that day was Indian baskets. They had many samples of baskets on loan from other museums to compare the work of Indians tribes from other areas of the country. Tasha made her way through the representational exhibits of housing and clothing. There were cases of artifacts and a short video. The museum was almost empty. She saw one older couple and a family with two little girls. Too bad, it was really a lovely little museum. She walked up the steps to the second level. The exhibit of baskets and containers on the second level was quietly exquisite. The staging, the lighting, and the soft music came together to make the exhibit truly exceptional. Tasha was glad she came. It was sad that more people were not there to enjoy it. She went through it twice, slowly.

"What do you think?" a man's voice asked.

"It's marvelous," Tasha replied, turning around to look at him.

"I am glad you like it."

He looked like he was about six feet tall, with softly curling brown hair and wire-rimmed glasses that framed light-blue eyes. He wore a tweed jacket, corduroy pants, and a khaki-colored dress shirt but no tie.

"It's a shame there aren't more people here."

"Well, we are a very small museum, but we have our moments. I'm the curator," he confessed in a very pleasant voice.

"And major contributing archeologist as well, I imagine," Tasha responded.

"Well, yes, but most of the digging for this exhibit was done online with other museums and private collectors."

"Well, it's wonderful. I love the way you have set up the displays."

"Thank you. Are you a professor at the university? You must be new. I know that I would have remembered you if you had wandered into my museum before."

Tasha laughed. "No, I am just a graduate student."

"Ah, graduate students, the lifeblood of the university pyramid system."

"I am not that kind of a graduate student. I neither teach undergraduate classes nor fetch and carry for professors."

"Well, that's disappointing. I teach one undergraduate class, and I have been searching for just the right person to fetch and carry for me." He smiled.

"I am working on a master's degree in clinical psychology."

"That probably doesn't leave much time for the care and feeding of simple assistant professors. You aren't, by chance, looking for subjects, are you?"

"Are you volunteering? How brave!"

"Well, I wasn't actually volunteering. I was just bantering."

"You are not a subject for analysis, then. How disappointing." She tilted her head to look up at him. "Still, your bantering skills are first rate."

"You are too kind."

A family with three children entered the exhibit area. The curator leaned down to Tasha and said in a low voice, "Would you be interested in seeing some of the uncatalogued items in the basement?"

They moved together out of the area and onto the stairway landing. "Is that rather like an invitation to view your etching?" Tasha asked.

"Oh no, I…" he broke off, his face slightly flushed. Then he looked at her and realized that she was smiling. "I just thought that since you enjoyed the exhibit, you might like to see some of the items that we didn't have space to display."

"I would love to." They spent the next hour exploring the basement of the museum. He was a wonderful guide, and Tasha thoroughly enjoyed the tour. His name was Luke Stafford, and he transferred there two years ago from a medium-sized museum in British Columbia, where he was an assistant curator. "I jumped at the chance to run my own museum. Plus, as an assistant professor, I have summers free to go on digs."

"What about the museum?" asked Tasha.

"Oh, I set up the exhibit for the summer and let the assistant curator run the show for three months." They worked their way back to the front of the building.

"I know this is rather brash, but would you consider having dinner with me?" he asked.

"I suppose I should demure since we only just met, but

I would love to have dinner with you," Tasha replied.

They agreed on Indian food for dinner, and Luke was also happy to attend the chamber music with her after dinner. He wanted to drive or walk her home after the concert, but Tasha was firm about leaving him at the museum steps. She went up on tiptoes and gave Luke a soft kiss on his cheek. She declined another dinner date for the next night, but she did give him her phone number. He was wonderful company, but he was too earnest for where she was in her life. And besides, he was probably at least ten years younger than she was. It was rather sad that she should meet such a lovely man when she wasn't really looking. But she was deliciously tired and ready for sleep.

CHAPTER 13

ON MONDAY MORNING, SADIE called. She rarely called, so that alone was enough to alert me, but the tone of her voice told me that something was really bothering her.

"Come over," my boss ordered without explanations. Then she modified it slightly. "Can you come over now?"

"Sure," I answered. "I'll be there in a few minutes. Are you OK?"

"Yeah, just come."

Sadie's yard looked as if someone had taken the contents of a huge dumpster and spread it all over. Her lawn was completely covered with trash. She met me at the door.

"Huge mess, isn't it?"

"I can't believe this! When did it happen?" I asked.

"Must have been last night 'cause it was here this morning when I let Sophie out."

"This is unbelievable. Have you called the police?"

"Right before I called you. They said they would be here

sometime this morning. I guess that's OK. Damn stuff's not going anywhere until we pick it up."

We went inside and made tea and cinnamon toast while we waited for the sheriff.

When he arrived about an hour later, he asked Sadie all the questions I already asked her. No, she didn't hear anything last night. No, she couldn't think of anyone who would do such a thing. And no, she didn't have any particular enemies. He shook his head, clearly puzzled.

"Usually, it's kids behind this kind of vandalism. But this is bigger than what kids normally do. And they usually target several houses or someone they have a grudge against. There were no other reports of vandalism last night on the entire island. I checked." He opined that it was one of a kind and would not be repeated. He also said that they would try to include her house on their nightly patrol for a week or so and to call him if anything else turned up.

"This is so strange. I just can't think of who would have done it or why," I said. I called Tina and she came over. She brought several large plastic garbage bags with her at my direction. It took us a solid two and a half hours to clean up the mess. Tina brought her husband's truck, and we threw the bags in. She said that Richard would take them to the dump when he went to work in the morning. Sadie didn't help, which was unusual. She did make us toasted cheese sandwiches for lunch. I expected her to be angry—I was. But she was strangely quiet. We all pretty much agreed with the sheriff's assessment that this was a onetime random act of vandalism.

The following morning, Sadie was ready when I picked her up. She seemed like her usual self, and we discussed the bakery offerings for October. I was planning on potato and pumpkin curry for soup selections. Sadie wanted peanut butter and Halloween-decorated sugar cookies. In addition to our usual cinnamon rolls, she was going to make pumpkin tarts and pumpkin cream cheese rolls.

We were ready for the month, and the first week went well. I really considered dropping lunch on Fridays. I thought that in the fall the lunch business might drop off without the summer crowd, but it didn't. Sadie said she didn't have an opinion about it one way or another, so for the time being, we decided to continue offering lunch on Fridays. She was letting me make more and more of the decisions about running the bakery. The nursery was closed for the season, and I still hadn't found another job. But the bakery was busy, and I could survive on that for now.

The closing on the bird farm property was set for the third week in October. Kat and Marla were coming into Seattle to spend the night at Peter's apartment. Peter's attorney also finalized the papers to incorporate the dog business. Peter was still not sold on the idea, but Kat was thrilled. The girls had plans to include pet boarding and obedience classes in addition to the breeding and selling of Doberman pinschers. Marla was going to move into the house as soon as the renovations were complete. Currently, she lived in a trailer on five acres of land located in the Kitsap Peninsula. The property's main feature was a large barn that Marla turned into kennels.

Marla was an American Kennel Club judge as well as a breeder and trainer. As a dog show judge, she traveled not only throughout the state but out of state and internationally as well. She made it clear that she was not going to be available to oversee the renovations on the new property. Peter felt strongly that even after the renovations were complete, a groundskeeper and manager would need to be hired. He figured that salary into the operating budget. His biggest challenge right now was finding a good general contractor to get the renovations started. Kat was bringing a list of potential candidates with her, and Peter would have Josh check them out before they were even interviewed.

The closing was accomplished without problems. The sleazy real estate agent Thomas Bohan was obviously not happy at Peter's insisting on using his own broker, but he showed up at the Seattle office on time and with all the correct paperwork. The man could not get out of selling mode. He kept saying, "You are getting a great deal."

Peter felt no need to answer him, but his sister finally replied in her soft voice, "Thank you, Mr. Bohan. We are very pleased with the property."

"Hey, I know a great contractor. He could do all those renovations you need to get the place operational." Bohan had made this offer before. Peter was going to tell the man that he would find his own contractor, but once again his sister answered.

"Oh, how nice of you. We would be happy to have his

name."

Peter knew what he would do with any name from this bozo, but Katelyn was right; there was no need to antagonize the man.

"Well, you got a great deal. Wish I could have been in a position to buy that property. It has so much potential." He wrote the contractor's name on the back of one of his business cards and handed it to Katelyn. He then gathered up his papers and left.

Peter took the girls out for a celebratory dinner. He wanted to ask Kat if she had seen Clair lately, but the dinner conversation was all about the plans for the kennels. From there it progressed to which of Marla's bitches were expecting puppies. Bitches made him think of Cynthia, which really wasn't fair. His former girlfriend was exactly what she always was, and that had been just fine with him. She wasn't a bitch, precisely, but when he thought about her, he was pleased that they were no longer together. He didn't call her after his last weekend on the island, and she didn't contact him either.

Peter didn't intentionally plan to miss the bank's symphony gala. He didn't intentionally decide to break up with Cynthia. That thought concerned him a little because he considered himself in total control of his life. Well, not total control. There were God and his sister, who often led him down unexpected paths. Thinking of unexpected paths brought his thoughts back to Clair. He tuned into the girls' conversation. They were discussing the breeding of various male and female dogs. He tuned out again.

Kat was up early the next morning. She was alone with

a cup of tea when Peter came into the kitchen for his first cup of coffee. He kissed his sister on the cheek. "Happy?"

"Divinely," she replied. "I never thought I could have this much energy again. I get up every morning full of plans and so excited to start the day. Thank you for making it all possible."

"Not me," he responded. "It was Mom and Dad's money that made the trust."

"I know and I am grateful to them as well. But you made it happen, my Saint Peter."

He sat down next to his sister with his coffee. He tried for a casual tone. "Have you seen much of Clair?" Katelyn put her cup down and looked seriously at her brother.

"No, I haven't." She paused. "Peter, haven't you called her?"

"No," he confessed.

"Are you unsure of your feelings toward her?" his sister asked, going right to the heart of the problem as always.

"She isn't my usual style."

"Thank God for that," she answered fervently.

Marla came into the kitchen, and that was the end of the discussion. Peter was both relieved and frustrated.

"I think I'll come up Halloween weekend," Peter said as he moved the girls' bags to the entry hall.

"Well, you can certainly come up, but Marla, Cerberus, and I will be at a dog show in Portland that weekend. Marla is showing one of her dogs."

Peter was a little surprised that Kat would be gone. Getting used to his sister in her new role as a dog breeder/businesswoman was going to take time.

"Don't forget to leave me that list of local contractors," he said.

"Do you want the name that Mr. Bohan gave me as well?" she teased.

"Nope," he answered. "I think you know what to do with that one."

"Maybe you should look at it just so we know which one to completely avoid."

"You know, little Kat, sometimes you have a great deal more business sense than I give you credit for."

CHAPTER 14

TASHA WAS SEEING LUKE more often than she should. He was great company, and they had so many interests in common. It was so easy to say yes to his calls for dinner, a concert, an art show, or a museum showing. Sometimes they just went for a walk in the park. One Saturday, the weather was so warm they rented a canoe and spent half the day on the marshy waterways behind the university on Lake Washington. Tasha knew that Luke was lonely and looking for more in a relationship than she was willing to give him. He would be perfect for Clair, but she long ago gave up trying to play matchmaker for her daughter. She tried to gently discourage any romantic inclinations Luke might have toward her. She never allowed more than hand holding and an occasional kiss or hug. Luke made it clear that he wanted more, and it wasn't that she wasn't attracted to him, because she was. Luke deserved to find a lovely woman and have a family. He deserved a chance to do all the things that she had already done, and she needed to find a way to encourage him to move past her.

Luke invited her over to his house for dinner. He and his Siamese cat rented a small two-bedroom house close to the museum. The cat, whose name was Isis, sometimes went to work with Luke. Tasha met her there once. Luke's house was dangerous territory, and Tasha knew she would have to have an honest discussion with him that night.

"That was, without doubt, the best pot roast I have ever eaten," she said, wiping her mouth with a napkin.

"Thank you, kind lady. I would love to lead you on, but honesty compels me to admit that it is almost the only thing I can cook."

Tasha tilled her head as if considering his confession. "Hmm, the only thing?"

"Well, of course I can cook fish; I am from British Columbia. Also omelets, and I make a mean pancake."

"I knew there was more. You are simply too perfect, Luke Stafford."

They cleared the table, rinsed the dishes, and loaded the dishwasher together. They also finished the red wine that Tasha insisted on brining.

"Let's go sit in front of the fire. The fireplace is the main reason I agreed to pay the outrageous rent on this house."

"Where's the bathroom?" Tasha asked.

"Down the hall, first door on the right," Luke directed as he moved to put another log on the fire. As she came out of the bathroom, Tasha stopped to look out one of the living room windows instead of joining Luke on the couch in front of the fireplace.

She felt the warmth of Luke's body as he came up behind her and slipped his arms around her. He felt so good. It would be so easy to sink back into his solid, warm male body. Tasha sighed; Luke tightened his hold and started to nuzzle her neck. She could feel the hardness of his desire for more than a platonic relationship. She turned in his arms as he lowered his head to kiss her, but she evaded his mouth. "Luke, we must talk."

Luke groaned but released her. He took her hand and started leading her toward the couch. "OK, just tell me that this isn't the 'let's just be friends' conversation."

"But, darling, you know it is. I am simply too old for you."

"Tasha—" Luke started to object, but Tasha needed to say it all first.

"If we stay together, one morning you'll wake up and realize that you want a marriage and a family. I have had my family, Luke."

"I have been married," he responded. Tasha was surprised, but she didn't answer. Instead, she titled her head as if asking him to go on with that memory. "I was married for two years. We were probably mismatched from the beginning. I wasn't exciting enough for her."

"And?" Tasha asked, encouraging him to continue.

"And she is now remarried to a hockey player on a second-string team, and I moved to Seattle and became a curator of a small university museum. End of story."

"No," Tasha answered. "Not end of story, Luke. It's just

the beginning of a new story for you."

"Tasha, I'm not looking for marriage right now. I know that you're divorced, and you are not looking for that kind of commitment now, either."

"That's true, but you tactfully left out the fact that I have two grown children."

"I am not interested in having a family."

"You might not be interested now, but tomorrow you may be."

"Then I'll deal with it tomorrow. I know you probably think of me as Dudley Do-Right, but I've had my share of women both before and after my marriage. I know that what we have is special. We would be great together."

"I don't doubt that you have had your share of sex. You are a very attractive man," Tasha said. "Luke, I adore you. I love being with you and spending time with you, and we probably would be great together. But we're at very different places in our lives, darling. If we allowed our relationship to include sex, then one morning you *will* wake up and realize that truth. We might both be deeply hurt."

"Tasha, I am a grown up. I understand the risks. Why can't we just have an affair, and when it's over, it's over?"

"It is over, Luke."

"It can't be over, because you never let it really start. And don't say I'll thank you in the morning because I won't."

Tasha got up from the couch. "I had hoped for a graceful exit, but I am not sure that's possible." Luke followed her to the entry closet and helped her with her coat.

"You could never be anything but graceful."

"And you are gallant as always."

"But good guys don't always win." He pulled her into an embrace and kissed her.

Tasha didn't remember how she made it to her car. It must have started to rain again because she had to wipe her eyes several times on the drive home. Funny, there weren't any raindrops on the windshield.

The next morning, Tasha had a serious discussion with herself. *I need to concentrate on my work. No more men. What about your decision to have some fun in your life?* She argued with herself. *Men could be fun. What about sex? There was that. All right, no more serious relationships. Sex is good, but friendships with men can be problematic. I handled the situation totally wrong last nigh*t, she thought.

CHAPTER 15

IT WAS NINE O'CLOCK on the eve of Halloween. There were no children on the beach this time of year, so I didn't anticipate any trick or treaters. I ate half a bag of Mary Jane peanut butter taffy and half a bag of candy pumpkins. I also built a fire in recognition of my mother's favorite holiday. I was watching *Halloweentown* for the third time and waiting for a rerun of *Hocus Pocus* to come on at ten.

Molly was asleep in front of the fireplace. Suddenly, she jumped to her feet and charged at the front door, barking madly before I even heard the knock. I flipped on the porch light and opened the door.

A very lovely gypsy and a roguish-looking pirate stood there.

"Trick or drink?" my mother and her pirate chorused.

"Mom?"

"Hello, darling." She bent to caress Molly, who was wild with joy.

My mother introduced me to Paul the pirate and invited him to get comfortable while we fixed drinks and snacks. Mom, Molly, and I adjourned to the kitchen.

Mom started fixing a tray of food. "Mom, who is that pirate?"

"I met him in one of my classes. Isn't he handsome?"

"Mom, it has to be unethical for a professor to go out with his students."

"Oh, he isn't the professor. Do you have any french bread?"

"No, but I have some brioche and pumpkin tarts from the bakery. You mean he is a student? At his age? That's even worse."

"Pumpkin tarts, yum. No, he is a psychologist. He was a visiting lecturer in one of my classes last month."

At that point my mom had put together an elegant selection of snack foods from my refrigerator and pantry.

We snacked, we talked, we drank, and we watched the movie. Paul, the pirate, was charming and fun. I also had to admit that he was very good looking. He probably wasn't thrilled with the movie, but the tradeoff was that he got to cuddle with Mom, and he took full advantage of it.

"Well, it is getting late, and you don't want to miss the last ferry." I couldn't believe I was saying this to my mother. Talk about role reversal.

"Oh, we aren't going back tonight. We have a room at the Captain Whidbey for the weekend," she answered.

"What? Mom, can I speak to you for a moment?" I dragged my mother into my bedroom. Molly came too. She was not letting Mom out of her sight.

"Mom, what are you thinking? He's just looking for a good lay."

"Yes, and he got one," she flashed back with a smile.

"I can't believe this. He just comes in and lectures to troll the class for victims. He's using you!"

"Trolls? Victims? How very Halloween, darling."

"Mom, I'm serious."

"I know you are, but Paul is not using me. If anything, it's a mutual arrangement."

"But…but, HIV, STDs—" I sputtered.

"My medical training may not be 'au current,' but it isn't exactly from the Dark Ages." My mother worked part time as a registered nurse when my brother and I were growing up. Her medical training and experience were what made it so easy for her to go after a master's degree in psychology.

"But, Mom, you always taught me to avoid casual sex."

"Did I? I may have been wrong."

The gypsy who used to be my mother drifted back into the living room. She picked up her pirate and left. Molly threw herself down in front of the dying fire and mourned. I ate the rest of the candy and felt sick.

"Shannon, I do not want to go the Trek's End tavern. I don't care if they do have live music and karaoke."

"Oh, come on. It'll be fun."

"I am sure that Nick would love having me tag along."

Nick was Shannon's longtime boyfriend.

"You know that Nick doesn't mind. Honestly, Clair, you have no social life. It's not healthy."

"I do too have a social life."

Shannon was my best friend, and I hadn't even told her about Peter. But what was there to tell, really? I hadn't seen Peter since the night we shared DVDs and pizza. The night we almost had sex. That night left me fantasizing about romance. Romance was a place I hadn't visited since college. I didn't have time for romance. And even if I did, Peter hadn't even called.

"Right, when was the last time you went out?" Shannon asked as she sorted through my closet.

"Molly and I went to the opening of the new off-leash dog park just last week."

Shannon groaned. "I hesitate to point this out to you in your currently deluded state of mind, but taking your mother's dog to a dog park opening is not in the viable realm of a social life. I rest my case."

"Shannon, I know you're trying to help, but my life is just too full of other issues right now," I protested. "I have no idea how to help Sadie or what to do about the bakery. My mother is rapidly regressing into adolescence, and I can't find another job. I don't have time for a social life."

"Here, wear this and the jeans and these boots." Shannon threw me a soft green sweater, a present from my mother.

I gave in, but I was terrified that Peter might show up any minute. My body was vibrating with tension. Nausea was crawling up from my stomach. I was continually scanning the tavern and refused every offer to dance. Fortunately, I drove my own car, and after a never-ending half hour, I mumbled an apology to Shannon and left.

On Sunday morning, Sadie called. "I've got a problem."

"Should I come over?" I asked.

"Yeah, I think you better."

"Are you sick or hurt? Do you need medical help?" Lately Sadie was looking fragile to me, and I was worried about her.

"No, it's the vandals again."

"I'll be right over."

I saw Sadie's problem as soon as I drove down her long driveway. There were two big signs stuck in her yard. One read "Get out now" the other said "Get out while you still can." All the bushes in the yard were toilet papered, and on the sloping roof of her garage was another message. It was spray painted in red—"GET OUT!"

Sadie met me at the door.

"Sheriff's coming over as soon as he can. Guess it was a busy Halloween night."

Both Sadie and the sheriff decided that this was just another incident of random vandalism. Tina and I weren't so sure. And the next week, another letter arrived in Sadie's mail suggesting that now would be a great time to sell because there was a potential buyer. The sender was unidentified, but the return address was the same post office box as the previous letters. Tina saved both the letter addressed to Sadie and the one she received. We both felt that Sadie was being targeted. We decided not to share our suspicions with Sadie.

I tried to find out whom the PO box belonged to, but

the post office said they didn't know, and even if they did, they could not share that information with me. Tina and I cleaned up the yard, and Tina's husband was supposed to clean off the spray paint from the garage roof.

By the second week of November, Tina got tired of waiting for him and did it herself. We didn't know where to go with our investigation from there, so we kept our worries to ourselves and kept an even closer eye on Sadie. Sadie seemed unconcerned about the vandalism and decided that the bakery would offer whole pies for Thanksgiving on a bigger scale than usual. We advertised in the local paper and took preorders. We had so many preorders that I decided to set a cutoff date. We would already be baking night and day. We were also offering monkey bread, which was a seasonal favorite. Visions of an expanded bakery where we could offer full Thanksgiving meals danced through my dreams, but in reality, I was up to my ears in pies.

CHAPTER 16

PETER HAD TWO GOOD candidates for a general contractor. November was probably not the best time to start renovating outdoor areas, but there was plenty to start on the inside. The girls were wild to get started, and Marla wanted to move in as soon as possible. Peter took Friday off so he could interview the two men. Interestingly, Josh was also going to spend the weekend at the beach house. Peter asked Josh to vet Mike Bell and Carl Jenson, the potential contractors, which he did. Neither had police records and both had good reputations, so there was really no reason for Josh to personally interview the two men. Peter was confident that he could select the man for the job. He did plan to have Josh's company install a security system on the house and the property, but that wasn't going to be needed for months yet.

It was very unusual for Josh to take an interest in such a minor matter. Josh said he needed a weekend off and he liked the island. He planned to stay at one of the B&Bs, but Kat invited him to stay at the beach house. They were going to drive up separately. The interviews were set for Friday afternoon, and they planned to meet at the property. Both Kat and Josh were there when Peter drove in. Kat had given Josh a tour of the grounds, and now they were going over the house. Kat was glowing with excitement. The interviews went well for both men, but Mike Bell could start immediately. Both contractors were invited to submit bids as soon as possible. Everyone agreed to dinner at Toby's, but Kat wanted to go home first to feed Cerberus. Josh said he would pick up his car later and ride with Peter to the beach.

Peter figured he wanted to talk about the interviews without Kat hearing, so he was surprised when Josh said, "I checked with the local sheriff, who said there've been several incidents of vandalism in the area recently. Sheriff says it is out of character for the neighborhood. We will want to get the security system up and running before anyone moves into the house."

They got to Toby's before the Friday night mob and snagged a large, round table near the front window.

"Let's go to Toby's for dinner. It's still early. Might be able to get a table." Mom was having a glass of white wine and a long conversation with Molly when I got home from the bakery on Friday afternoon. She called earlier in the week and asked if she could come up for the weekend. Of course, as the week progressed, I totally forgot.

"What, no pirate?" I asked, dropping into a chair across from her.

"No, the good thing about pirates is that they come and go with the wind. Anyway, I'm off men. I need to concentrate on my studies."

That's a relief, I thought. "OK, sure, Toby's is fine. Just let me take a quick shower and change my clothes."

Toby's was full but not packed when we got there. Still, it was Friday night, and there were no tables available. There was one seat at the bar, and Mom and I grabbed it.

Peter looked around the room both hoping and fearing he'd run into Clair. He still hadn't called her, and he wasn't sure why. He couldn't get her out of his thoughts, and she took up way more space in his head than he wanted her to. Kat and Josh were talking about the renovations. Peter noticed that Josh had some excellent suggestions.

Kat was enjoying Josh's company; he had some great, practical ideas, and he paid attention to what she said. Suddenly, she felt her brother tense beside her. Peter seemed to be lost in his own thoughts that night. He added very little to the conversation at the table. Kat scanned the room and saw Clair at the bar with someone who had to be related; they looked so much alike—an older sister or perhaps even her mother. Her mother! Of course, they met her clamming on the beach. Kat was sandwiched in between her brother and Josh. She couldn't easily get out, and she didn't want to yell across the room.

"Peter, look. Clair's at the bar. Why don't you invite her to share our table? There's plenty of room."

"She's with someone," Peter replied.

Josh picked up on Kat's intention. "We can make room for two more."

"It's her mother. Remember we met her on the beach?" Kat added.

Peter moved with his natural grace around the pool table and toward the bar. Clair saw him coming and tried to hide behind her mother. Peter observed her maneuver and countered by pretending to approach Tasha only. "Hello, I'm Peter Cameron. We met on the beach this summer. My sister and I have that large corner table. Please join us."

Peter pointed toward the table where Kat was waving at them.

"Oh, how nice. We would love to." Tasha walked toward the table. Peter waited for Clair to move away from the bar.

I was fervently asking the timing gods to slip me into another dimension when I saw Peter walking toward me. As usual, there was no celestial response. He reached out to take my beer off the bar and carry it to the table. "Of all the joints in all the world…" I muttered.

"Yeah, yeah, I know I should have called. But I have been thinking about you."

"Oh, that makes me feel so much better." I grabbed my beer from him and walked ahead to the table.

Josh remembered the girl from the bakery. There was definitely some tension between Peter and this woman. Her mother was certainly attractive, and he wondered if she was as feisty as her daughter. Introductions were made, and food was ordered. Kat glowed with excitement as she explained her plans for the old bird farm property.

Tasha sat next to Josh and tried hard to remind herself that she had sworn off men at the moment. But the man next to her was making it difficult. He looked good. He smelled good. He had a strong, mellow voice, and when his hard thigh accidentally touched hers, her stomach did a flip.

Josh was trying to concentrate on Kat's conversation, but the woman next to him was distracting. She was lovely, and that was not an adjective Josh used for his usual women. He couldn't stop looking at her. The scent of her was driving him wild, and he almost vaulted out of his seat when their thighs accidentally touched.

Peter was trying to share in his sister's enthusiasm, but he kept getting lost when he looked at Clair. He wanted to sit next to her. Hell, he wanted to touch her. But he stayed in his seat next to his sister on the outside of the half circle and kept his mouth shut.

I didn't want to be at the same table with Peter. I definitely didn't want to sit next to my mother. *Why didn't Peter call me?* I couldn't feel anything from him—not love, not hate, not disgust, not amusement, nothing, nada, a large blank. He was decidedly a large male blank that I wanted to fill in. I thought about making up an excuse to move across the table and into his lap. Well, maybe not his lap, but at least next to him. On second thought, maybe into his lap would be good. Maybe it would be great.

I knew that I shouldn't order another beer. Three beers put me in a dangerous time zone, and this would be my fourth. Things around me slowed way down except for my tongue, which gained a life of its own, one that was entirely unrelated to my brain. We finished our fried clams and chips. It was my favorite meal, and I didn't taste a thing. I ordered more drinks. My mother challenged Josh to a game of pool, and I grudgingly moved to let them out. They were having way too much fun, and Peter still had not spoken directly to me. I moved in to sit next to Kat, and we talked about dogs.

Peter brooded. He was very conscious of the conversations going on over and around him, but he was not motivated to become involved. He watched Clair, remembering how she felt and how she tasted. This self-proclaimed time-challenged woman was becoming a challenge for him.

Josh was surprised that Tasha could actually play pool. She came close to breaking even with him. But her laughter and the sound of her voice were distractions, and the way she moved restricted his movements. His jeans were tight and almost uncomfortable. It had been a long time since a woman affected him this way. To Josh, women had become a disposable commodity. Two ex-wives were more than enough. Fortunately for him, both remarried, and Dominic was his only child. Well, the only one he knew about. His son turned out to be a good man and a good son. The credit should probably go to his mother, although Josh stayed married to Monique for most of Dominic's formative years.

"Where did you learn to play pool?" Josh asked Tasha as they returned to the table.

"My son taught me," she replied as she moved behind the table to sit next to her daughter.

Josh pushed in beside her. He draped a casual arm around

her shoulders and then removed it.

"My mother does everything well," I heard myself say.

"Oh dear," Mom said in a soft undertone, sensing a verbal avalanche that she did not know how to stop.

"Unfortunately, not all things are genetically transferred." Oh no, my tongue was on a roll.

"I know what you mean," Kat joined in, trying to make this a conversation. "Peter has so much more financial ability than I do." She flashed a loving smile at her brother.

"I got all the worst genetic traits: fizzy hair, carbohydrate intolerance, and big breasts and bottom," I said in a gloomy, sodden tone.

"Hey, some of us happen to appreciate breasts and bottoms." Josh tried to lighten things up. But my tongue would not be silenced.

"I also inherited terrible timing and a tendency to pick up stray animals."

"Not to mention a low tolerance for alcohol," Peter added.

"Hey, you're not a part of this conversation," I snapped at him.

"I think you inherited good qualities too. What about intelligence, a sense of humor, and a loving nature?" Kat put in.

"You forgot a cold, wet nose," Josh added.

"Hey, you're not part of this conversation either," my tongue slashed at him.

"On that recurrent note, I think it is time for us to fade into the sunset." Mom stood and took my arm. Josh moved to let us out. Suddenly, my brain caught up to my tongue, and I grew silent. *Why are the timing gods always tardy when showing up in my social situations?* I wondered morosely. We stopped to pay our bill at the bar, and Mom drove us home. Once again, I totally humiliated myself in front of Peter.

Tasha was up early the next morning. Her dreams were full of Josh. She was a free woman of a certain age. Not only had she grown up in the age of feminism, but she was on her way to being a psychologist. Sex was a natural human need. Sex didn't embarrass her. After all, she just had a very satisfying affair with a pirate. But her dreams of Josh were absolutely embarrassing. And she was certainly, beyond a doubt, not going to do anything about those dreams except stuff them away. She was positive that the man was a menace to women. And besides, she'd sworn off men for the moment. She trudged out into the kitchen with Molly at her heels. She filled the coffee pot with water and reached for the coffee beans. No! It was simply not possible. Her daughter was a work in progress, but she was not irresponsible. She couldn't be out of coffee. Tasha searched every cabinet without finding a backup coffee supply.

She pulled on a pair of jeans and a sweater and drove to Prairie Center Mart. On the way back to the beach, she saw a sign with the shadowy outline of a dog and an arrow, proclaiming "Sheepdog Trials."

Maybe it was the lack of caffeine in her blood or the lingering sexual frustration that made her decide that watching canines chase sheep would be the perfect way to spend the day. It would get her away from the house and off the beach. It was the perfect activity to keep her from running into Josh.

"Are you sure you don't want to go? It is such a beautiful day." Mom tried for several minutes to talk me into going with her to the sheepdog trials. "We could pack a picnic lunch."

"Only you, Mom, would want to pack a picnic lunch in November on the island. And, yes, I am absolutely sure that I do not want to go. After last night, I am unwilling to subject any other human being to my company."

"You weren't that bad. In fact, I think Peter and Josh were rather amused."

"Unfortunately, that isn't the first time I have amused Peter. And that is not exactly the emotion I am trying to elicit from him. Do you think I have a drinking problem?"

"No. You rarely drink, and you know you have a low tolerance. I think something else is bothering you. Do you and Peter have a history?"

"No! No history and definitely no future," I replied.

"A day outside might help."

"No, Shannon gave me some ideas for online employment that I want to check out."

"I am going to watch the sheepdog trials this afternoon. Do you want to come?" Kat ask Peter.

"Ah…tempting, but *no*."

"You mean you are not even tempted?"

"Afraid so. I am not even remotely tempted."

"Marla has some friends who raise Australian shepherds. They are not as good as border collies at herding, but they're still pretty impressive. We may want to add another breed if the kennel does well."

"I'll go with you, Katelyn, if the offer extends to me." Josh had just come into the kitchen for his second cup of coffee.

"Oh, Josh, I would love to have your company."

"You better pack lunch. She won't remember to feed you, and you'll be miles from any kind of civilization," said Peter, who had plenty of experience with his sister's outings.

The sheepdog trials were miles and miles away from any town. The signs led Tasha down roads and into places she didn't even know existed on the island. Finally, a gravel road led her to a flat area with a sign that said "Park Here." It was already full of trucks and trailers. She and Molly walked up a dirt drive to a large grassy area. The actual trails were held in a fenced pasture, which was on a gentle slope with a flat area at the bottom. Outside the fenced area, people clustered in groups with lawn chairs, thermoses, and dogs on leashes. The trials were already in progress. Tasha was fascinated seeing the dogs maneuver the sheep through the gates and turn them into pens. The dogs and their handlers were awesome, and the communication between them was amazing. Molly collapsed at her feet, totally unimpressed at the sight of such canine prowess. Tasha watched several trials while leaning on the pasture fence and wishing she thought to bring a chair. Since Molly was so disinterested in the proceedings, Tasha dropped the end of the leash.

Suddenly, Molly exploded off the ground and under the

fence. She ran up the hill with her leash trailing behind her. The working dog gathered the flock into a nice wedge and was herding the sheep down the hill toward the first gate. Molly ran right into the middle of the wedge. The sheep scattered like balls on a pool table. The sheepdog was momentarily confused. Should he go after the sheep or the large black furry beast? Tasha climbed the fence in a heartbeat and ran after her dog. Molly thought that this was wonderful fun. She was thrilled that her favorite person decided to join the game and took cover behind various sheep. The handler wisely called her dog to heel, reducing the chaos slightly. Fortunately, this was a placid herd. Molly was totally insane, but the sheep always suspected this about dogs. Tasha tried to grab Molly's leash as she ran circles around her owner and through those wonderfully smelly white things. Tasha lost her balance on the slope and almost fell, but she stepped back into a wall of male body, and a strong arm came around her waist to steady her.

"Don't chase," she heard a deep voice whisper softly in her ear. Oh no. It couldn't be. As if her position weren't humiliating enough. Tasha closed her eyes and told herself to take a deep, cleansing breath. What she breathed in was not fresh, bracing air but the unmistakable scent of a clean, strong male. She knew that scent, and it inspired her with the wildest urge to take off all her clothes. That was just ridiculous. She was centered, she was calm, and she was a professional. Damn, she felt as wild as her dog. What in the world was Josh doing at the sheepdog trails? He turned her around and casually reached down to grab the end of Molly's leash. It wasn't obvious to those watching, but he managed to touch her body all the way down. A spontaneous cheer came from the spectators.

"My hero," Tasha spit out.

"Do my ears deceive me? Is that sarcasm? Shall I let loose the hound?"

"No!" Tasha screeched. "I am grateful, honestly. I am just so mortified that I was momentarily bereft of an appropriate response. I don't understand it. She's not a sheepdog; she's a water dog." They started down the hill.

"Hmm, that *is* confusing. Perhaps she is having an identity crisis." Josh chuckled as he helped her over the fence, keeping a tight hold on the unrepentant dog's leash. Kat met them on the other side of the fence. She was trying hard not to laugh.

"Oh, Katelyn, I am so embarrassed. Should I pay some kind of damage fee?" Tasha asked.

"No, the sheep are fine. No harm done. These are dog people, so they understand; just keep a tight hold on Molly's leash." Speaking of keeping a tight hold, Josh was having a hard time taking his arm off Tasha. He found that he wanted to keep it there. In fact, he wanted to put his other arm around her. In fact, he wanted to—no! He was definitely not going there—at least not in his waking fantasies.

The big black-and-brown Doberman sat quietly beside Kat. He tipped his head slightly to the side and looked at Molly as if to say, "What possessed you, girl? That was unbelievably bad dog behavior."

"Molly and I are going to slink home now with our tails

between our legs. I cannot believe how badly she behaved. I think I may have been too permissive with my fur child," said Tasha.

"My partner Marla is going to be giving obedience classes," Kat offered.

"Sign us up," Tasha said as she took the leash back from Josh and pulled her recalcitrant canine toward the parking area.

My friend Shannon had been getting email job offers. That was not uncommon. Nurses were hard to come by these days. But one of the offers was for online counseling. It was a twenty-four-hour backup service for an expensive weight-loss program. The job did not require any kind of medical background and only asked for a college degree. Shannon thought I might be able to sign up for an evening or night shift and still do the bakery. Or I could sign up for the weekends. Anyway, it was worth a try. My resume was up to date, so I spent about an hour composing a brilliant cover letter and sent both off via the internet. Now the rest of the day loomed in front of me. Molly went with Mom to watch other dogs herd sheep. Why would my mother not believe me that Molly needed serious training? I loved Molly, but I learned the hard way not to trust the impulsive beast. It was definitely a mixed blessing having her as my housemate.

It wasn't raining, which was a plus for November on the island and far from a given. I called to check in on Sadie.

Tina stopped by that morning, so she was fine and didn't need anything. I put in a load of laundry and contemplated cleaning a bathroom but decided against it. If I put if off long enough, Mom would probably do it. I decided that a walk might be good. I walked down the beach but the tide was in, so I couldn't get around the point. The house next to Kat's was empty. Most of the houses on the small peninsula of land were used only during the summer. I cut through the yard and onto the gravel road and then back to the beach. When I was out of sight of all the houses, I sat on some drift logs and contemplated the water. It was gray, with slow, steady waves and occasional white-capped bursts of energy. *A bit like my life*, I thought.

Peter saw her walk through the yard next door. Without any clearly formed intention, he put on his shoes, grabbed a windbreaker, and followed her. He caught up with her when she stopped to sit on some drift logs.

"May I join you?" he asked.

Clair shrugged her shoulders.

I hadn't expected to see Peter. I was still mortified by my previous night's repeat performance at Toby's Tavern. Of course, it was my usual bad timing, so I should have anticipated it. Peter sat next to me. He didn't talk. He was just there, a strong, solid presence. After a few minutes, he put his arm around me. It felt wonderful. I leaned against him just a little. He moved his hands up to frame my face and kissed me. I just dissolved into the kiss and the feel of his hands on my face. We seemed to be outside of time. From somewhere in the fog, I heard him say, "I can't seem to keep my hands off you."

"Don't."

"Don't what?"

"Don't keep your hands off me."

"Wait, you want me to stop?"

"No, don't stop." It was the one thing I was sure of in this timeless space.

CHAPTER 17

MIKE BELL LET HIMSELF into the house on Sunday afternoon. He won the bid as general contractor to renovate the buildings on the old bird farm. It was a huge job, and he was excited about it. It came as a blessing for him and the men who would be working with him. The good-weather jobs were over for the year. There were always odds jobs around, but a long-term, solid project like this one was surely a gift. He started going room to room, making notes on a clipboard. Katelyn Cameron and her brother would join him in about an hour, but he wanted to get a feel for the house and the outbuildings first. He was reviewing his notes when he heard them drive up.

Mike was a little surprised to see that they had another man with them. Peter introduced the other man as Josh and identified him as a security consultant. They were going to want a security system on both the house and the kennels. Security systems were not unheard of on the island, but the area was considered very safe, and most people didn't even bother locking their front doors. Whatever they wanted was fine with Mike. He didn't do security systems. Together, they went through the house and the outbuildings again. Mike made more notes on his clipboard. Josh also took notes. Mike thought that he could have the house livable by January, but the outbuildings were going to need extensive work, and the fencing was best left until the spring. Kat's partner, Marla, was anxious to move in, but she couldn't do that until there was also housing for the dogs. Kat knew that Marla would want to start on the outbuildings first and leave the house until later. But Peter was adamant that the house be renovated first. Mike thought that he could run two teams, one in the house and another on one of the larger outbuildings for the kennels. He could also enclose an outside exercise area for the dogs if the weather permitted. But even with two teams, he estimated mid-January for a move-in date and that was with the understanding that people and dogs living there would have work crews in and out for many months after that. Peter was also insistent that no one live on the property until the security system was in place. Mike figured that Peter was just overprotective of his sister. Josh was obviously a professional, and Mike would have no problem working with him. They reviewed Mike's plan for the week. He left to line up a crew for the next morning. Kat went back to the beach house to call Marla. Peter and Josh returned to pack and take the ferry back to the mainland.

On Monday evening, Tasha called her daughter. She thought maybe they could have Thanksgiving at the beach this year. She had no classes after Tuesday morning. She could come up Tuesday afternoon, shop Tuesday evening, and get most of the baking done on Wednesday. Clair could invite Kat, Peter, and Sadie. She tried hard not to think about Josh being invited. She and Luke were back on speaking terms, and she might invite him. But she couldn't get Josh out of her mind. She had only met the man twice, and she was dreaming about what it would feel like to make love to him. *Get over yourself, Tasha*, she admonished herself.

On Monday afternoon at the bakery, Tina and I baked pies. We didn't tell Sadie. I was afraid that if we didn't make a head start, we would never be able to fill our preorders. I was tired by the evening when Mom called. I pleaded tired when I hung up and realized that I just agreed to my mother's Thanksgiving drama with a cast of thousands. I hadn't really considered what I was going to do. I guess I would have gone down to Mom's for dinner, loaded up on leftovers, and watched *A Charlie Brown Thanksgiving*. It wasn't really fair to call Mom's idea a drama. She just had all this crazy, natural energy. If I was being honest with myself, I liked the idea. It was a win-win situation for me. It was a chance to see Peter again. Sadie and Mom got along great together, and I really liked Peter's sister, Katelyn. In an uncharacteristic burst of social aptitude, I called Kat and invited her and her brother. She accepted and asked if she could bring her business partner, Marla, and maybe Josh.

"Absolutely," I assured her and told her to call any others she wanted to. I knew that Mom's theory of entertaining included gathering all stray people in any given area. Kat said that she did not cook, so she could not offer to bring food, but that Peter was great at wine, and they would bring red, white, and some nonalcoholic choices. Sadie was strangely enthusiastic about my offer. She said that she had not been looking forward to spending the day with Tina and her family. It was a strange thing for Sadie to say because she loved Tina, but when I thought about it, she had never really liked Tina's husband. Sadie suggested that we snag some pies and monkey bread from the bakery for our feast. "Great idea," I said, "that will really cut down on what Mom has to cook."

Mom came up Tuesday afternoon as scheduled. She checked in at the bakery. We were slammed trying to fill all the Thanksgiving preorders, not to mention all the people who just stopped in to pick up whatever they could get to add to their feasts. Lunches were cancelled for the week, so the front tables were free. I took a tea break, and we sat at number four to plan. Tina waved and Sadie came out to give Mom a hug and tell her that we saved pies and monkey bread for our own celebration. I think Mom was relieved not to have to do all the baking, but with her it was hard to tell sometimes. She revised her shopping list, and we compared the anticipated guest list. She then left for power grocery shopping in Oak Harbor, and I went back to the cash register. Tina took Sadie home for a nap.

On Wednesday afternoon, I was so exhausted I could barely drag myself home. I did remember to bring the monkey bread, the pies, and a large box of cinnamon rolls. Mom set the table. She had one of her Celtic CDs on loud, and she and Molly were cooking something in the kitchen. I checked in and went to change my clothes. I didn't plan on napping, but I must have because when I woke on my bed, it was dark and the house was silent. *Note to self: no more brilliant preholiday order ideas,* I thought. *Well, we at least need more help if we decide to do it for Christmas.*

I didn't need to think about the bakery and the upcoming Christmas season. I needed to think about what I could do to help Mom with Thanksgiving tomorrow. I checked my alarm clock. Nine o'clock! I couldn't be. It was. There was no sign of Mom or Molly. A few lights were strategically lit throughout the house. A note on the kitchen counter confirmed that they were in bed.

"I will be up at zero dark thirty to put the turkey in the oven. Planning feast for about one o'clock. Sleep well. Love, Mom."

There was also a schedule indicating what times and temperatures various dishes needed to go in the oven. I thought about eating, but reading the schedule made me faintly nauseous, so I decided on a glass of water and a quick return to my own bed.

The production was flawless. Kat, Peter, and Josh arrived at about noon. They brought cases of wine, beer, nonalcoholic sparkling cider, and bottled water.

"I hope you don't mind that we brought Cerberus," Kat said as the large male Doberman followed her in.

"Of course not. Molly will be thrilled," Mom replied

without a moment's hesitation. She was equally as composed when Marla showed up, just as we were placing the food on the buffet, with a large female Doberman and six puppies.

"We're weaning," she explained, "so I couldn't leave them." The puppies were settled in the laundry room, and the mother dog joined the other two adult canines in front of the fire. "They still have to nurse every four hours, but she needs time away from them too," Marla continued.

"Of course," Mom replied, "no problem." And it wasn't. I picked Sadie up just after noon, and Mom's friend Luke arrived while I was gone. The food was fabulous, and amazingly, the group around the extended table was as totally compatible as the dogs. Mom mentioned earlier that her friend Luke might join us. Of course, I had no idea that her friend was closer to my age than hers. I had to admit that he was charming. If I hadn't been so distracted by Peter, I would probably have been thinking evil thoughts about my mother.

Kat was disappointed that Josh's son, Dominic, hadn't come. She met him several times and found him extremely attractive. Apparently, he was opening a European branch of the security company and was spending most of his time overseas. Josh offered his son total control of the American business, but Dominic wanted more of a challenge.

Josh had to agree that his business ran smoothly. He chose exactly the right people to manage the three main offices in Seattle, Denver, and Dallas. He decided when he originally set up the business that the East Coast and California were already saturated with security firms. He would concentrate on the Northwest and part of the South. It worked out well, and his business had a great reputation and continued to grow. Josh understood Dominic's restlessness. He was also getting faintly bored with the operation. The income was excellent and steady, but it was rare that his teams couldn't handle anything that came their way. They stayed current on technology and threats. They picked their people carefully and didn't overcommit their resources. Josh felt free to give into the momentary diversion of Peter's current project. He liked the island and was more than willing to be distracted. He also hadn't had a steady woman for a while. If he was honest with himself, and he tried to be, he was also bored with casual sex and one- and two-week affairs.

The table conversation was mostly about the proposed kennel and the plans for the renovation, but they were a diverse group and willingly stretched to discussions of tidal rights, current events, and which wine best complemented the turkey. There was universal agreement that dessert would be postponed for at least an hour. The only problem this presented, as Tasha saw it, was for Luke. Peter and Josh were spending the weekend with Kat. Luke was the only one who had to catch a ferry back or drive the long way around. Tasha was pleased when Luke had accepted her dinner invitation. She hoped that this evening would solidify their relationship as friends. She enjoyed Luke's company and would have loved for him to be attracted to her daughter, but it looked like Clair was focused on Peter. She wasn't sure if Peter felt the same. Well, at least today Luke had a good feast and companions that were his own age. She was concerned about him driving back tonight and chalked it up to her maternal instincts. She brooded over the problem as she loaded the dishwasher and transferred food to plastic containers. She bought many disposable containers for leftovers and planned to send everyone home with doggie bags.

She went to the laundry room to retrieve more containers that she had stashed on top of the dryer, totally forgetting about the six puppies contained there. The puppies had been sleeping, but about half an hour before dinner was completed, they woke up. They were bored and hungry. With very little effort, they knocked down their pen and spread out to investigate the laundry room. When Tasha opened the door, they were ready to make their break. Six sleek little furry bodies streaked out.

"Let loose the hounds," Josh proclaimed. He was covertly watching Tasha. He liked the way she moved. Two puppies headed for the kitchen. Two headed for the table, making jumps to grab whatever smelled so good on that surface. One went directly to his mother who jumped to her paws, and one dashed back to explore the bedrooms.

Marla let out a bellow. Peter, Clair, and Kat fended off the puppies who were jumping at the table and were underfoot in the kitchen. Josh rescued the wine bottles that threatened to overturn when the tablecloth was caught in puppy mouths. Molly jumped to her paws and started racing around the room barking. Sadie was laughing so hard she could hardly catch her breath. Luke looked on at the situation with bewilderment. Tasha was mortified. How could she have forgotten that the puppies were in the laundry room? Marla and Kat started gathering up the puppies and putting them back into the laundry room. The mother dog meekly and, with just the hint of a sigh, sank onto the floor in front of the dryer to nurse her family. Peter continued to clear the table. Tasha walked carefully through the kitchen and the chaos and went outside to the deck.

Cerberus remained sitting calmly in front of the fireplace. During one of her random, wild circles through the room, Molly ran right into Marla as she was coming out of the laundry room. Marla's face was white, and she grabbed Molly by the collar. "Sit!" she thundered, and Molly did. She then instructed the unrepentant but sobered water dog to lie down, which, amazingly, Molly also did.

All but one puppy was safely enclosed and peacefully nursing. Luke found the last puppy under the bed in the guest bedroom. He handed it to Kat, who followed him down the hall. She gathered the puppy closely to her and held it, breathing in its scent. Luke watched her as she cradled the little animal and bent her head down to breath in.

"Thanks," she said, flashing him a glowing smile. Kat laid the puppy next to its nursing brothers and sisters. She stood watching them for a few minutes. Marla appeared to be guarding the door when Kat came out of the laundry room.

"I think those puppies are ready to be fully weaned."

"Yes," Marla acknowledged. "I started them on some solid food yesterday."

"Athena looks worn out," Kat ventured.

"She has been a good breeder and a good mother. This will be her last litter," Marla answered. Kat knew that Marla was an excellent breeder and that she was good to her dogs, but a slight misgiving entered her heart.

"Seems a little heartless, doesn't it?" Luke said as they walked back toward the table.

"Yes, it does. That beautiful creature is more than just a good breeder and a good mother," Kat answered, looking around to be sure that Marla had not overheard their conversation.

Josh filled two glasses of Pinot Gris and followed Tasha out onto the deck. Tasha accepted the glass he held out to her and gave her head a slight toss.

"You are just trying to make up for that 'let loose the hounds' remark."

He laughed. "Guilty as charged."

"I can't believe that I forgot those puppies were in the laundry room. I need either less of this or a whole lot more." She held out her glass to toast. Josh touched his glass to hers with a smile.

"Mind overload," he opined.

"Not me. I thrive on minutiae. I am the queen of multitasking," she responded.

"Over organized?" he threw back.

"Are you hinting that I might be just a tad controlling?" Her light laugh took any challenge out of the question. Josh raised one eyebrow in answer. "Is that a polite way of saying that I am totally compulsive?"

He laughed. "I don't think that I have ever been labeled as polite in my entire life."

They looked out at the bay with a surprisingly peaceful silence between them.

Dessert was fabulous, and the remaining afternoon went as if it were scripted. Both people and dogs were pleasantly full and calm. Marla wanted to go up and see the bird farm property, but it was too late in the day for that. The light was quickly fading. She and Kat leashed Cerberus and Athena, the mother Doberman, for a walk. Luke volunteered to take Molly.

"Are you sure?" Tasha asked. "She is terrible on a leash."

"Terrible is a slight understatement," I added.

Surprisingly, Molly accepted the leash and walked demurely out the door behind the two Doberman pinschers, with one large brown canine eye always focused on Marla. Upon their return from the walk, Tasha was relieved to hear that Kat persuaded both Marla and Luke to spend the night. Her beach house had a room off the garage, which would be perfect for Marla and the dogs, and there were two double beds in the room Josh was using. Josh agreed, and it was settled.

On Friday morning, Marla was anxious to see the property before heading back to the peninsula. She loaded Athena's crate in the back of her van and put the mother dog and her puppies inside. Luke wanted to see Chief Snakelum's grave. It was supposedly located close to the bird farm property. He mentioned it last night. I was there years ago and volunteered to show him where I thought it was. Kat said she wouldn't mind going if we could wait until Marla saw their prospective place of business. Josh quietly told Peter that he didn't think the girls should go over to the property alone.

"A quest!" Tasha labeled the outing, but she declined to join.

"I wonder why Tasha didn't come," Kat said. She and Clair were riding together. Luke was driving himself because he was going home after they explored the gravesite. Peter and Josh were also driving themselves because they were Peter and Josh. Marla and her dogs were in their van.

"She probably wanted to rearrange the cheese drawer of the refrigerator," Clair answered bitterly. Kat was surprised by her new friend's comment.

"I didn't realize you didn't like your mother."

"Not like her? Not like Tasha, the perfect woman? Of course I like her. It's just that I don't want to grow up to be her."

Kat suddenly understood that right now, it wasn't her mother Clair didn't like; it was herself.

Kat didn't comment on her insight into her new friend's mind. Instead, she said softly, "I wish I had known my mother better. She wasn't around much when I was growing up. My parents kind of abdicated their parenting role, and Peter took over. I still don't understand why." She paused. "I know that's why he's so protective of me."

They pulled into the parking area. Both women looked over at Peter, who was standing by the perimeter fence talking to Josh.

They walked through the house and the outbuildings that were still intact. They were pleased with the early progress. Several walls in the house had been removed, along with all the carpet. Marla decided to let Athena have a run before the long drive home. She and Kat put the puppies in one of the old bird runs where the fencing was almost complete. They stood guard by the one area that needed repair. Cerberus and Athena took off joyfully down the center path between the old bird pens. The rain was holding off, but the wind was coming up, and leaves blew up against the old netting. Clair walked over to where Josh and Peter were standing. The contractor already started work on a large fenced exercise area. The men were apparently reviewing the work. Josh bent down and picked up a letter-sized white piece of paper. Its white presence stood out glaringly from the dried brown leaves that had blown up against the old section of fence.

"Oh, those damn flyers!" Clair blurted out as she saw what Josh held.

"What are they?" Peter asked, a little surprised at Clair's tone.

She explained how both Sadie and Tina received numerous letters just like the one Josh was holding.

"Someone's trying to buy up property in this area?" Josh asked.

"Apparently," Clair responded. "I wonder why they didn't bid on the bird farm property."

"Maybe they did," Peter said. "The agent said there was another bidder. I just figured he was trying to raise the price."

Why would someone want to buy in this area? It doesn't even have a water view, Josh thought, but his train of thought was interrupted as Marla started up her van and Luke and Kat walked over to join the group. Luke was eager to find the Indian grave before the weather broke. Peter and Josh opted to return to the beach house.

Clair led the way down a well-worn path just outside the bird farm property. They walked for about five minutes and then turned onto another path through a meadow that ran in front of Sadie's house. As they walked into an overgrown wooded area, the path became less traveled.

"I can't remember if it is off to the left or the right," Clair admitted.

Cold blasts of wind penetrated the tree cover, and a light mist began to fall. It was still morning, but the overcast sky wasn't providing much light. Clair arbitrarily turned to the right. Kat and Luke followed. After about five minutes, Clair was sure she turned in the wrong direction. Crashing through thick underbrush where no path existed, they worked their way back to the original turning point. Now the rain was starting to fall in a serious manner, and Kat was visibly shivering.

"I think we better start back to the cars. Now that I know the area, I can come up and explore it on a better day," Luke said.

"I am so sorry. I know it's around here someplace. I thought I could walk right to it." Clair admitted defeat and turned her small party back toward the bird farm. They were soaked by the time they reached the parked cars. Luke planned to drive home, but Kat convinced him to come back to her house and change out of his wet clothes.

"Maybe if the weather gets better, we can look again this afternoon." Kat liked happy endings, and she could see that no one was happy with this one. Clair was still in a beastly mood, and Luke was obviously disappointed about the failed search. The afternoon was cold, and a steady rain settled over the island. After a lunch of mandatory turkey sandwiches, Luke decided there was not going to be a magical weather change and left for home. Kat pressed a small piece of paper into his hand.

"Call us when you come back to explore the gravesite," she said as she and Peter walked him to his car.

CHAPTER 18

THE FIRST WEEK OF December rushed by, and I still had still not decided whether the bakery was going to take preorders for Christmas, as we had for Thanksgiving. We did well financially, but the labor was intensive, and I was uncertain about doing it again so soon. Sadie said I could do as I pleased and that she didn't care one way or another. Tina also seemed to be ambivalent. The nursery closed for the season, and I had not found another job. Sadie insisted on a raise so I would be able to pay my monster electricity bills and feed myself. My mother left Molly with me but continued to pay all the dog's expenses. I immersed myself in the day-to-day workings of the bakery. We continued the Friday lunches and offered seasonal favorites like mincemeat pies and eggnog cheesecake, but we didn't take any preorders. It wasn't so much that I made a decision but rather that I just let things happen by default. Instead of taking orders, we increased the volume and let each week's demand dictate the followings week's production. We sold out almost every day.

Mom bought tickets for *The Nutcracker* ballet. She called and invited me to come down on Friday evening so that we could shop for a Christmas outfit on Saturday before the performance. It was a holiday tradition when I was young, but we hadn't attended the Christmas ballet for years.

I didn't want my mother to buy me a dress-up outfit, and I wasn't sure about going to the ballet, although I did love it. Finally, I agreed to go to the performance but declined the shopping opportunity. If Mom was disappointed with my decision, she didn't show it. Molly and I arrived on Saturday afternoon. Mother seemed happy to see us and had lunch ready. After lunch, we took Molly for a run in the park. The performance was going to be in an old theater, which was recently refurbished. For dinner before the ballet, we decided on a small Indian restaurant that we both liked in the University District.

"The theater has been redone in art deco. Luke said they did a great job," Tasha said over chicken tikka masala

"I'm surprised that you were able to get tickets for any performance this late. I remember that they were always in November. I know this because, with my usual lack of timing, when I started thinking about Christmas last year, it was mid-December, and I couldn't find a *Nutcracker* production anywhere."

"You are absolutely right," replied Mom. "They held off this performance because they wanted to spotlight the theater revamp. I bought the tickets months ago when I read about it. It is actually the only holiday thing I have done this year.

I just can't seem to get in the spirit."

I noticed that my mother had not decorated the apartment. That was very un-Tasha-like behavior. In fact, when I looked closer, it didn't seem like Mom decorated for the fall season either. The apartment was clean, but it looked like an unfinished photo shoot. Mom collected old eighteenth- and nineteenth-century picture frames. She used them as decorative accents, and there were several on the fireplace mantel, but they were empty. They would usually be showcasing scarecrows or angels or any number of items that Mom collected and artfully displayed. I remembered fall as my mother's favorite time of year. My childhood memories were full of scarecrows, pumpkins, friendly ghosts, and witches. These icons of the fall easily moved into the angels and Madonna, highlighted with greenery and the spiraling white lights of the Christmas season. Was something wrong with my indomitable mother? I pushed the thought away. Nothing could be wrong with Tasha. She dressed up for Halloween as usual, if just a bit excessively, in my opinion. And she orchestrated the Thanksgiving banquet. Now she bought tickets for *The Nutcracker*. Nothing was wrong with my mother. All was right with my world, and I realized that I was looking forward to the ballet.

Kat and Cerberus had been at Peter's apartment in Seattle since the first week of December. After the death of their parents, Peter insisted that Kat spend every holiday with him. That was fine with her, and in all honesty, she needed a break from the beach house. The weather was cold and wet on the island. Usually, she could load up on books, light a fire, and be perfectly happy, but this year, she was feeling restless and maybe even a little lonely. She stopped by Clair's a few times, and once they went out to Toby's for clams, but Clair was busy with the bakery, and Kat had days and days of wet and gray. So she and Cerberus were happy to move into her brother's penthouse apartment for a few weeks.

Peter was at work during the day, but there were museums and art galleries to visit. She even went to see Luke's museum in the University District. Luke found her halfway through the first floor and insisted on giving her a guided tour. He also invited her out to dinner. They tried to get Tasha to join them, but she had an evening class. Peter also declined; he said that he needed to get some extra work done so that he could take some time off. True to his word, Peter spent all of Saturday morning exploring the farmers' market with is sister. It was one of Kat's favorite places.

"Look, a tarot card reader!"

Peter groaned. "You know those things are a pure scam."

"Think of it as entertainment if you want to," Kat responded, dragging him toward the small stall under the stairway.

"Romance has entered your life, but you resist it," the woman told Peter. Her cards predicted that Kat's current project would prosper.

"What a bunch of…" Peter didn't finish his statement because he saw his sister's expression. She was glowing. He would do anything he keep that smile on her face.

They stopped for clam chowder at one of the little restaurants on the street level.

"I have a surprise for you," Peter said, "but you have to guess."

"I'm having such a wonderful time! I can't believe that things could get any better. You'll have to give me a clue," Kat exclaimed.

Peter started humming the theme from the dance of the sugarplum fairies. It was a game they played when Kat was young and one that got her through hours of pain in various hospital beds. He would hum some classical music, and she would have to guess the name of the piece and the composer.

"Too easy," she laughed. "Tchaikovsky, *The Nutcracker Suite*."

He smiled. "Right, and we have tickets for tonight."

"Oh, Peter. That's so wonderful!" Kat jumped out of her seat and hugged her brother. "You are the best brother."

"Yes, and as the best brother, I'm taking you home for a nap." Kat's lupus seemed to be in full remission, but Peter wasn't taking any chances. Kat saw the shadow of responsibility in his eyes and wished her parents hadn't laid such a heavy burden on him. She knew that she was strong enough to take care of herself now. Some corner was turned; some door opened in her life. She couldn't put it into words, but she felt it strongly.

Once they were back at the apartment, Peter even volunteered to take Cerberus for a walk while she rested. She let him because it was easier. Thinking about easier led her to wonder about her brother's love life. There was no sign of Cynthia this time. That certainly made Kat's visit easier. She was reluctant to ask her brother about the status of his relationship with the femme fatale. Kat did not like Cynthia, and it was fair to say that the feeling was mutual. Kat was not jealous of her brother's girlfriends. She wanted Peter to have a woman in his life. But she was convinced that Cynthia was not that woman. The intensely controlling Cynthia was probably just as convinced that she *was* that woman. The fortuneteller said that romance was in her brother's future. Did that mean he was free of Cynthia's claws? Kat definitely felt something between her brother and Clair…she drifted off into the nap that she swore she didn't need.

The theater was magnificent. It was full of Christmas magic. Greenery overflowed out of huge iron urns, and fairy lights were everywhere. The audience was decked out as extravagantly as the setting. Little girls floated by in long burgundy dresses. The gilded mirrors in the entrance reflected their satins and velvets. Little boys dragged their feet, pulling at their suits and whining about the tightness of their shirt collars. But magic was thick in the air, and even the little boys would soon be caught in its web.

I was almost sorry I didn't let my mother buy me an outfit for the occasion.

"Oh, how wonderful…how perfect," Mom breathed at my side.

I had to agree that the setting was absolutely perfect. We moved with the tide of people up the ornately carved central double staircase to our seats in the first-row balcony. It was our traditional place. We tried to take in the magnificence of the theater. The Olympian gods and goddesses were there, painted on the ceiling. There were torches and cupids on the walls. The seats were red velvet and matched the beautifully draped curtains on the stage.

I felt Peter before I saw him. The male presence that was settling into the seat next to me felt familiar. We turned to look at each other at the same moment.

"Peter?"

"Clair?"

Astonished and delighted greetings were exchanged all around.

"Magic," Kat murmured.

"Synchronicity," Mom echoed under her breath with a smile.

CHAPTER 19

JOSH SETTLED THE NOISE cancelling earphones over his ears and closed his eyes. What the hell was he doing on a flight to Paris at Christmastime? The airport was, as predicted, a zoo. He liked Paris and had fond memories of France, but he had long since learned not to dwell in memories. He was a present-tense person, even after he transitioned himself out of warrior mode. He lived in the now. Memories could be treacherous and distract you from what was happening around you. As a solider, if you were distracted, you might forfeit your life or, worse, one of your teammate's lives. You trained for the future, but you didn't live there either. And it was the now that was becoming problematic for Josh. Holidays were always difficult for him…so Paris it was.

Dominic, his son, didn't need him. The new branch of the business was going well in Europe. He accepted that his son would not come back to live permanently in the United States. That left the management of the stateside business to

Josh, which didn't worry him. He had a solid organization and good people in middle management.

He wasn't concerned about accidentally seeing his former wife, Dominic's mother. He and Monique long ago worked out their differences. He even met and approved of her current husband. Josh liked Paris, but he wasn't sure he was in the mood for the beauty of the city. Sometimes beauty and romance demanded something from you. He was feeling restless and empty, and he hated the thought that a situation might ask from him what he could not give. *Well*, he told himself, *I will enjoy the city of lights for a week and a half, spend a day or two with my son, and then return to my home in the great Pacific Northwest.* As the plane leveled out and reached its cruising altitude, Josh drifted between a light sleep filled with dreams and recent memories.

"Relax, big boy. I'm not after your money, only your body," Tasha purred.

"What makes you think that I have money?"

"Oh, maybe that vintage Jaguar you drive."

Josh snorted. "It's vintage because I have had it so long. It's even older than your Mercedes. And if I had loot, what if I've already spent it?"

"Loot?" Tasha laughed. "Yes, I knew you were a pirate. That's perfect. I just want to use you for sex."

"Be still, my raising main sail. If I am a pirate, what are you?"

"I am working on becoming a gypsy."

"OK, gypsy queen, let's blow this scene."

"Ah, now?"

"Do I detect some hesitation? What about your blatant sexual invitation?"

"Well, I am kind of a gypsy in training."

"OK, let's go work on your gypsy skills. You know, I once knew a horse named Gypsy."

Tasha's face blurred in his memory, and he was free to dream a new, more personally satisfying ending to the scene.

I asked Tina to work extra hours, which she was happy to do. Sadie said she didn't care if we decided to close the bakery during Christmas week, or not. I didn't think we would have too much business if we stayed open, and I also felt that we could all use a rest. So it was decided that the bakery would be closed for Christmas week, and signs were dutifully posted. This would be the last day of operations for the bakery in this year. We would open again the second week of the new year.

Lunch was over, and Sadie was safely home and hopefully napping. Tina and I loaded the first dishwasher full of lunch plates and put some of the baking pans to soak. We sat with mugs of spiced apple drinks at our favorite table. The fog lay close to the shore, and the view out the window was a misty, floating soup.

"Sadie's still letting you clean her house once a week and pick up groceries, right?" I asked.

"Yeah, but she won't let me sort out any of those book boxes, and they just keep piling up. And once a week isn't enough to keep up with the needs of that house," Tina replied.

"What about twice a week?"

"She won't go for it. I already tried. I have to keep making up excuses to stop by. You know, to drop off leftovers or borrow something I don't need."

"I know. I do the same thing. I try and get her to go to Toby's with me for dinner or borrow a book or search for a recipe we could use."

"I know her daughter wants her to come for Christmas, but she flat out refused. Said it's too much effort."

"Speaking of Christmas, is your son going to get leave?" Tina's oldest son was in the army.

"No, but I'm real proud of him 'cause he passed this test, and he's going to be trained for some kind of water treatment work. He doesn't want to stay in the army forever, so he looked at what kind of training he could get a job with on the outside. He thought about working on motors, cars, and stuff like that at first, but when he looked into it, there were lots of guys doing that. He gets to come home this summer for a visit before he starts his classes."

"That's great," I said. "I know that you weren't too thrilled about him going into the service."

"I wasn't, but I think it may have been the right thing for him. He's smart and he thinks things through. Deloris does that too." Deloris was Tina's daughter.

"Is she still working as a nurse's aide at the hospital?"

"Yeah, but that friend of yours, Shannon, she's been talking to Deloris about singing up for the LPN program. You know, licensed practical nurse. She thinks she might be able to help her get a scholarship or a grant."

"Tina, that would be great."

"Yeah, she and Jeff want to have a baby in the worst way, but they're going to wait until they can afford a house. It's my youngest, Zach, who's driving me crazy."

"He dropped out of school, didn't he? Is he still doing odd jobs?"

"When he can find them. He's hanging out with a bad bunch, just trouble waiting to happen." Tina let out a deep sigh.

"I thought his dad was going to get him part-time work at the dump."

"He talked about it. Richard's good at talk, but it seems the county won't hire him even part time without a high school diploma."

"What about the GED program at the library?"

"He flat out refuses." Tina let herself be worried for a minute and then asked, "What are your plans for Christmas?"

"I haven't really thought about it." That wasn't strictly true. I was, of course, going to spend Christmas with my mother. "Well, I think I'll get a head start on the morning's baking. I feel like making gingerbread people and animal cookies."

"Clair, tomorrow is Saturday, and we are closed next week."

"Right. I just thought I would do some baking for our regulars and maybe take some stuff with me to Mom's." With my usual poor perception of time, I hadn't, on a conscious level, actually acknowledged that next week was Christmas. Now I accepted the panic that came with that consciousness.

Suddenly, my plan to bake that evening didn't seem so crazy. I stayed at the bakery until almost eight o'clock in the evening.

Molly complained loudly about her late dinner. I fell into bed, visions of baking sheets and tart molds left soaking in the bakery sink running through my head. I took Molly with me to the bakery the next morning. As if I didn't have enough to worry about, Treacherous Tasha invited Kat and Peter for a New Year's Eve celebration at her apartment. A celebration of the new year was particularly objectionable for the time challenged. It brought to mind all that had not been accomplished in the past year and all the bad karma that might have accumulated. It made a person face a space of exactly delineated time. A year—time that was marked out by intellectual agreement. It was definitely not my favorite time.

Molly and I arrived at Mom's apartment on Monday afternoon the week of Christmas. I brought gingerbread people, mincemeat tarts, and monkey bread. She wasn't home. I had a key, but I didn't go in. Instead, I took Molly on a long walk in the nearby park. Mom's car was in the garage when we returned.

"Hello, darling." Mom came out of her bedroom, a room she totally redid when she moved in. She asked permission since the apartment did actually belong to me. Since I had already redone the main bedroom in Tasha's beach cottage without asking, I could hardly deny my mother the same opportunity. Tasha gave me a warm hug and then bent to give one to Molly, who was visibly ecstatic at being reunited with her main person.

Uncharacteristically for Tasha, there were boxes stacked

up all over the living room and on the dining room table.

"Do you need help unloading the car?"

"No, I can get it." It took me only two trips to unload the car, one for my duffel bag and one for the bakery items.

"Oh, you brought goodies." Tasha sounded thrilled when I set the bakery boxes on the kitchen counter. She inspected the contents of the three boxes and sampled several gingerbread people. "These are wonderful! Can we eat the monkey bread for dinner? I made beef and barley soup."

"Sure."

We ate at the big, round kitchen table. It sat in a bay window overlooking the apartment's large backyard. Molly gobbled her dinner already and was sleeping blissfully under the table at Tasha's feet. She had made it clear that she was not letting Tasha out of her sight anytime soon.

"I love this soup," I said.

"I love it too. It was one of my mother's favorites. So many things remind me of her," Tasha added.

"Does that make you sad?" I asked. I was surprised at my own question, since I did not often think of my mother as being subject to common human emotions like sadness.

"Well, yes, sad and grateful. She gave me—us—so much. I guess I will miss her forever."

"My mother, the therapist, would tell you to concentrate on the grateful part and the sad part will fade eventually."

"How wise," Tasha responded.

After dinner, we moved into the living room, and Tasha lit the fire. "I'm afraid that I am way behind schedule this year. I just haven't been able to get in the Christmas spirit." She gestured to all the piles of boxes. "I hoped," she continued, "that you might go through the Christmas decorations and help me sort them out."

"I noticed that you don't have a tree this year."

"Well, Luke was going to help me get one, but then he found a really good last-minute fare and decided to go home to Canada for Christmas."

"Are you saying that you can't have a Christmas tree without male assistance?"

"No, certainly not. It's just that I'm more motivated to enact the Christmas rituals if I have someone to share them with."

"OK, let's get a tree tomorrow." I surprised myself with the suggestion.

We spent a peaceful evening sorting through Christmas decorations, remembering past years and choosing what to keep and what to let go. I went to bed feeling warm and secure. I had that feeling low in my stomach that I rarely got anymore. I felt safe and cared for. I used to call it the "home" feeling. I hadn't felt it for a long time.

The next morning, I woke to the smell of coffee and french toast. I wandered out into the kitchen to greet Molly and my mother. Coffee and a few good tail thumps from Molly helped wake me up. French toast was one of my favorite foods, and I never made it for myself. I wandered around the apartment, drinking coffee and reviewing the piles of saved ornaments. I noticed a guitar propped up in the corner of the living room.

"Isn't that Ben's old guitar?"

"Um…yes," Tasha responded distractedly.

"Where did you find it?"

"I was going through the basement a few months ago."

"Why did you drag it upstairs?" I remembered when my brother decided that he was going to be a rock star. My father refused to indulge the fantasy; loud rock music was not allowed in the house when I was growing up. Tasha bought him a good used guitar and started him with classical guitar lessons. That was a compromise, acceptable to both my father and my brother, for widely different reasons. The thought that my father had rather restrictive ideas of what was appropriate and what was inappropriate was not a new one to me.

My mother, I realized, was open to most any kind of creativity and was willing to nurture it in any form for her children. The guitar phase lasted only about six months, but my father made my brother stick with the lessons for a year. As I remembered, my brother soon progressed onto his martial arts phase.

"I'm taking lessons," Tasha answered vaguely. She was setting the kitchen table for breakfast.

"You're taking guitar lessons?" Why should I be surprised? Lately, mother's regression toward adolescence was escalating.

"Yes. I did ask Benjamin if I could use his guitar."

I knew that her mother kept in touch with my brother. They emailed each other at least once a week, and he phoned her often. I rarely corresponded with my brother. We led such different lives.

Tasha seemed disinclined to continue the subject. "Are

you ready for the great Christmas tree adventure?"

We had planned to leave Molly in the apartment in hopes that the tree would fit in the back of my small station wagon, but her mournful howls made Tasha change our plans. A delighted Molly was loaded into the back of the car.

It was three days before Christmas, and most of the lots were sold out, closed, or offering a very poor selection.

"These trees are just too Charlie Brown," I observed.

"Do my ears deceive me? What happened to our morning agreement that we would not obsess over finding the perfect tree?"

"Yes, well, there is a great deal of difference between the perfect tree and these pitiful offerings," I responded.

Tasha didn't answer. She was happy to spend the day outside with two of her favorite beings. She did smile at the thought that her daughter, who just that morning delivered an impressive lecture on the need to avoid obsessive behavior, was opting to continue the tree search.

Of course, including Molly in the adventure made the search into a challenge of animal management. She wanted to be involved in every step. Unleashed, she would run through the lots, knocking over trees and imprinting her doggie signature on them. In the car, she leaned heavily on Tasha's shoulder from the back seat, occasionally leaving a trail of dog slobber.

Despite the challenges, we decided to drive north of the University District and found the perfect tree late in the afternoon. We stopped at an Ivar's and picked up clam strips for dinner.

I agreed with Mom's decision to pay extra and have a wooden stand fitted to the tree. Still, by the time we unloaded it and found the perfect place to put it in the apartment, we were both pleasantly tired.

Christmas was surprisingly peaceful and beautiful. Tasha was, at that time, attending a small Episcopal chapel close to the university, and the Christmas Eve service was lovely. Even I, who resisted all organized religion, had to admit that the candle-lit service evoked feelings of sacredness, peace, and hope in my heart.

A few days after Christmas, I wanted to run back to the island. Christmas was unexpectedly wonderful, and I didn't want to spoil my mellow mood. Instead, I found myself helping Tasha prepare the buffet for the evening. I hated New Year's Eve celebrations.

"I can't believe you did this. You know I hate New Year's."

"I know, dear, and I appreciate your help."

"Who's coming?"

"A few friends from some of my classes, Katelyn, Peter, my guitar instructor and meditation guide, Luke, and maybe Josh if he's back. No more than fifteen people total."

"Josh?" I knew who Josh was. He was, as Sadie described him, a "hunk-a hunk-a." And he was at their Thanksgiving dinner, but I wanted to hear how my mother would describe him.

"Yes, he is the security-expert friend of Peter's. You remember he came to the beach cottage for Thanksgiving? Kat told me that he went to France to spend part of the Christmas season with his son. I understand that his second ex-wife was French, although I think she has been remarried for some time."

I groaned. "Not another one."

"Another what?"

"Mom! It isn't always about another man!"

"You are so correct, my darling daughter, but I think it may be about the love, the romance—it can be a dog, or a garden, or the perfect loaf of bread, or a child, or a poem. Anything that ignites the energy of life within us. This world is so full of possibilities."

"So, this Josh is a possibility?"

"No," my mother answered with a sigh. "Well, maybe..." she smiled and winked at her outraged daughter.

"Why should we celebrate the new year?" I asked Kat grumpily.

"Why not?" Peter was carrying a bottle of champagne and offered to refill both our glasses.

"I think celebrating is important and something that we don't do enough," Kat said, declining a refill.

"Mom would certainly agree with you. She believes that we should not only celebrate realities but also possibilities," I replied as I let Peter refill my glass. His hand brushed mine, and I felt the tingle all the way up my arm.

"I like that idea," Peter responded. "I agree with Kat and your mother that we should celebrate more often. Celebration is a statement of gratitude."

"Maybe it's not a celebration. Maybe it's a mourning of the past year."

"It depends on your perception of reality or your attitude or your belief system. You can be thankful for the things in the past year that went well or taught you an important lesson. You can anticipate good things happening in the coming year."

Kat decided that Peter could certainly hold his own against Clair's negative reflections. She drifted off to talk to Luke.

"Good things happen to people with good timing," I continued glumly.

"Ah, I remember you consider yourself time challenged."

"Yes, and as someone with good timing, you couldn't possibly understand."

"Oh, I understand. It's your personal version of victimhood."

"What?" I was outraged. "You, with your attitude of love 'em and leave 'em, dare to accuse *me* of being a victim?"

Peter shook his head. He put down the half-filled bottle of champagne and his own glass. He took the glass from Clair's hand and set it beside his own. He circled her right wrist with his hand and put a little pressure on it. She followed him down the hallway. He stopped in front of a slightly open bedroom door. He released her wrist and cupped her face with both hands. Giving her time to draw away, he leaned toward her and kissed her softly.

I hesitantly returned his kiss, so he kissed me again. I heard myself let out a soft moan.

"I think I might care for you more than you care for me."

"I don't think so," he whispered in my ear.

Tasha was in the kitchen refilling a silver tray with more salmon. Molly was right next to her, hoping for a small—or, preferably, a large—morsel to come her way. Josh wandered in behind her, carrying the empty bowl that was once filled with dill sauce. Tasha had no idea that he followed her. As she turned away from the refrigerator with a container in her hands, she walked right into him. "Oh, sorry, I didn't know you were—"

He held out an empty bowl.

"Thank you," she managed. Tasha was surprised that she didn't know someone followed her into the kitchen. She was usually very much aware of the presence of others. She did admit to herself that this particular man unnerved her. She tried to lighten up her own reaction to having Josh in her kitchen.

"Are you stalking me, or do you just want more salmon?"

"My actions are purely altruistic," he answered in a mock wounded tone. "More salmon demands more dill sauce. It's very good."

"Thank you," she responded, taking the bowel from him. "Somehow, I just don't see you as the altruistic type."

"No? How do you see me?"

"Well, I guess I would classify you as a predator."

"And do you identify yourself as prey?" he asked, moving just barely out of her way but still very much in her personal space.

"No," she answered firmly, "I stopped being prey a long

time ago."

"You think so?" he asked with a slight smile.

"I know so. I have been working very hard to be more than a small, quivering ball of warm fur."

"Interesting," he responded, reaching around her to grab a bite of fish. "You know, predators can smell prey even through their avowed denial." He rinsed his hands and wiped them on the hand towel Tasha pointed to.

"What you smell is fish. Here, fulfill your altruistic ambitions and put this back on the sideboard." She pushed the refilled silver platter of salmon into his hands and turned to wash out the bowl he had given her.

As he walked further into the kitchen, Josh kept up the banter.

"You know, we predators are persistent."

"Well, your instincts are off this time," she said as she walked out of the kitchen with the refilled bowel of dill sauce.

"I don't think so," Josh answered in a low voice.

Kat was telling Luke about all the progress being made on the bird farm property. Tasha joined them. "Do you think you will be in by January?" she asked Kat.

"No. Mike, the general contractor, is really pushing it, and the house may be ready by the end of January, but the outside spaces will probably not be done until late March."

"I know it must be hard to wait," Tasha sympathized. "Marla told me how anxious she is to move in."

"Yes, she is, but she won't move in until she can bring all the dogs with her, so that means waiting until the outside buildings have been renovated. Luke, did you ever get back up to see Chief Snakelum's grave?" Kat asked, trying to bring him back into the conversation.

"No, but I still want to see it. Are you still up for the adventure?" he asked.

"Definitely," Kat responded. "Call me when you are coming up to the island."

Tasha's party of fifteen people max turned into twenty. Tasha always made extra food, so feeding the small horde, as her daughter referred to the guests, was no problem. The large rooms were comfortably full, and the occupants seemed to be amazingly compatible. She drifted from group to group, sometimes joining in on the conversation, sometimes just checking that everyone had food and drink and that no one was left out. She saw Clair and Peter return to the group. Clair's face was flushed.

I was determined to leave early next morning, but I woke up late. The kitchen was totally clean. There was no sign of the party from the night before. Neither mother nor Molly was in the house or the backyard. *So much for getting an early start*, I thought as I poured myself coffee. By my second cup, mother and Molly had returned from the park.

"Hello, darling," mother greeted me as she hung up her jacket. I noticed that small droplets of moisture sparkled in my mother's hair and her cheeks were pink.

"Mom, I really wanted to get an early start this morning."

"Oh, are you all packed?"

"No."

"Ah. Were you waiting for Molly?"

"Not really. I just can't seem to get moving. I am so busy

when the bakery is open. I don't have to think about what to do or when to do it. Things have to get done, so they do. I guess I just need outside stimulus to keep me on time. I always feel like I'm wasting time when I'm not at work."

"You are not, darling. Time is just a concept. It can be a friend, or you can make it a foe. Fear makes it your enemy. There is no power in time itself, only in your perception of it."

"This from a woman who is in perfect control of her time."

"Clair, I am not. But I have learned that what I fear controls me."

"I am going to pack."

I declined her mother's offer of lunch. I loaded my stuff in the car and came back one last time to get Molly. Tasha passed me the leash. "I think I'm going to have to come up and get Molly for a while."

I felt a tightening in my chest. Molly was a pain and I resisted having her stay, but now I realized that I would miss the dog dreadfully if mother took her back. I swallowed hard. "Do you want me to leave her?"

"No. I'll be up in a few weeks to pick her up."

"OK." I gave my mother a long hug.

CHAPTER 20

THE LAST WEEKEND IN January brought a break in the weather. People who lived on the island of wet and gray knew they better take advantage of light and sunshine when they were blessed with it, so they poured out of their dwellings. The malls emptied out, and the beaches and parks overflowed with pale people and happy hounds. Luke sat in a ferry line that stretched beyond his sight line. He understood the ferry traffic routine. He brought a snack and some reading material. He was amused to watch his fellow travelers; some turned off their car motors and got out of their vehicles. They walked their dogs, talked with other pilgrims, and made sorties to the small kiosks lining the road. Others were glued into their driver's seats, nervously tapping on their steering wheels, voicing their discontent to fellow travelers, and occasionally jumping out of their cars to peer over the offending vehicles ahead of them in line. Luke could see the questions in their straining bodies and seeking eyes. "Was the ferry broken, run aground? Were those idiots running only one ferry? Why hadn't they moved at all for thirty minutes?"

Luke was patient by nature, and as diverting as the human nature around him had been, he was happy to finally drive across the shaky metal ramp onto the ferry. The trip across the sound was as refreshing as the wait was tiring. Luke stood on the upper deck of the ferry and let the cold wind sweep over him. He wondered what the native people saw when they crossed to the island in their small boats.

He called Kat before he left, and she agreed to meet him. She was already there when he pulled into the old bird farm parking area. Although it was a Saturday, Mike Bell and his crew were hard at work on the main outbuilding.

"I am so glad to see you. Did you have to wait a long time for the ferry?" Kat saw Luke pull in and walked up to meet him as he got out of his car.

"An eternity, but it was worth it. The ride over was glorious," Luke replied, bending down to greet Cerberus.

"Clair is coming with us. I hope that's OK. She felt like she had to redeem herself after the last time."

"Sure, that's fine," Luke answered.

Cerberus barked once, and Clair's old station wagon appeared as if on cue.

Clair got out and quickly opened the back door behind the driver's seat, reaching in to leash Molly. Molly bolted out the door and dragged Clair toward the big male Doberman pinscher.

"I'm sorry, but I had to bring her. She's been shut in for days, not that she minds the rain. She loves wet in any form."

Molly greeted Cerberus enthusiastically.

"Oh, it's fine. Cerberus will love having the canine company," Kat answered with a smile.

Luke also smiled a greeting. "All are welcome on this journey," he said.

"I talked with Sadie," I said as we started walking through the field beside the kennel property. "She gave me a better idea of where to look."

Kat let Cerberus off his leash when they started to walk. Molly was dragging me. "Do you think I could let her loose?" I asked Kat.

"Do you trust her?" Kat asked.

"Not at all," I answered. "But I think she'll stay close to Cerberus, and he comes when he is called."

Kat laughed. "Well, I think you will make a better guide if you are less encumbered."

I removed Molly's leash with relief.

The grave, when they found it, wasn't much. It consisted of a large stack of rocks with shells and pebbles arranged in a circle around it. Inside the circle were more shells arranged in various undistinguishable patterns and some bird feathers tied to sticks that were pushed into the ground outside the circle.

Luke seemed happy with the gravesite. "Chief Snakelum was most probably not buried anywhere near here," he observed.

"But it is lovely that he is remembered," Kat said as they stood quietly outside the circle.

"Yes, he wasn't famous like Chief Seattle, but he was the documented chief of this area," Luke agreed.

Clair added, "I like that our little spit of land was named after him." It was quiet in the woods around the grave. Even Molly was reserved. As we turned to walk away from the gravesite, a large blue heron flew over. The bird let out a raucous screech.

Luke looked up and smiled. "Just checking in," he said, nodding. They stopped walking for a minute to follow the bird's flight. "Birds are thought to be messengers from the departed." Luke's voice was deep and vibrant: "The white man will never be alone. Let him be just and deal kindly with my people, for the dead are not altogether powerless."

After a moment Kat said, "Chief Seattle, right? I remember that quote from one of the displays in your museum."

"Very good. Full marks!" Luke smiled at her. The three of us and out two dogs seemed completely at peace with the world and each other as they walked back across the field. Before they reached the parking area, Kat called Cerberus to her side and attached his leash. She stood quietly with the big dog sitting calmly at her side while I snapped on Molly's leash. Molly sat because her hero, Cerberus, sat. She seemed somewhat surprised when I walked up and attached her leash. Well, she was a little tired, anyway, so she didn't protest it.

Kat urged Luke to stay on the island for dinner. The three of us went for an early meal at Toby's Tavern. Kat offered him the guest bedroom, but he left right after dinner, preferring to deal with the shortened ferry lines Saturday evening would bring rather than the endless lines guaranteed on Sunday morning.

The tavern was starting to fill up, so we decided to go to

my house for dessert. "I have blueberry pie from the bakery," I offered as incentive.

"How can I refuse?" Kat answered. Once at my place, we settled into chairs, looking out toward the water.

"Shall I light the fire?" I asked.

"Not for me. I'm very happy right here. This pie is fabulous."

"Thanks, it's a favorite at the bakery."

"I am so impressed with the way you run the bakery, Clair, not only the baking but the business end of it too."

"Sadie has taught me so much. Almost all the recipes are hers; I've only made a few small changes."

"How is she doing?" asked Kat. "I know you've been worried about her."

"I have. Her heart doesn't seem to be in the bakery anymore."

"Are you worried that she'll sell the business?"

"Oh, Katelyn. I hadn't even considered that."

"I'm sorry. I didn't mean to give you one more thing to worry about."

"No, you are right. I should have considered it. I just assumed that the bakery and Sadie would always be there. That they would be there as long as it took me to decide where I wanted to go in my own life."

"I suppose I should be worried about whether Marla will stay with me in the dog business. She might change her mind after all the work is done on the property."

"Yes, but you are in a much better financial position, aren't you? I mean, you own the property."

"I do own the property, thanks to my parents' money and my brother's oversight, but Marla has the dogs and the knowledge. The business wouldn't work without her side of it."

"I guess neither one of us is as secure as we thought," I sighed. "We can't control the future."

"I used to be terrified of change," Kat said softly. "But something inside me just shifted during my last hospitalization. It was the sickest I'd ever been. I spent months in and out of the hospital. It turned out to be the best time in my life. I learned so much. The doctors finally diagnosed me with lupus. I met Cerberus, and I learned to trust. Now I know, not just believe but *know*, that change is just change."

"You mean you can survive whatever change brings?"

"More than that, Clair. It's more than knowing that I can handle whatever changes life brings me. It is trusting that the change, in the long run, will be positive for me."

"You are an optimist."

"Perhaps." Kat knew that it was more than that, but she couldn't explain it to Clair. Clair would have to learn it in her own way and in her own time.

CHAPTER 21

FEBRUARY ON THE ISLAND could be dismal. But for Kat and Marla, it was wonderful. The house was complete. The largest outbuilding was totally remodeled, and Mike Bell and his team were working hard on the others. One large section of fencing was in place, and Marla agreed that it was enough for her to move in with the dogs. A caravan of friends with trucks and vans volunteered to move the dogs. Peter rented a large truck for Marla's furniture, and Josh volunteered to help. He spent the last week installing a security system on the house and ordered two of his people from the Seattle office to install a separate system on the outbuildings the following week. He wasn't happy about not being able to put in a comprehensive system for the entire property. That would have to wait until all the outbuildings were completed and the inner and outer fences were in place. Kat would stay at the beach house and spend her days at the new kennel property. They decided to name it Bird Farm Kennels.

Marla agreed that she wouldn't continue using her old kennel name since they would be sharing the dogs bred at the new property. She was well enough known in the dog world that the name change would soon be common knowledge. She was also confident that they would be producing champion show dogs in one year under the new kennel name.

The move started in the dark hours of Saturday morning. Peter and Josh drove the rental truck up to the peninsula on Friday afternoon. Peter didn't understand why Josh was willing to involve himself so much in Kat's dream. He could easily just send one of his teams to install the security system for the kennel property and be done with it. He didn't know what was motivating Josh, but he enjoyed the older man's company and was grateful for his advice.

They loaded the rental truck with all of Marla's possessions. Now, in the cold and misty hours of the morning, a procession of trucks and vans moved silently toward the old barn that Marla was using as a kennel. Peter and Josh set up a card table with the coffee and cinnamon rolls Kat insisted they bring. Then they stood by and watched. These were dog people; they knew what they were doing. Their quiet, precise movements spoke of countless long mornings and tired nights spent loading crates and animals in just the right arrangement to fit the assorted vehicles and canine temperaments. Dog shows meant loading and unloading animals and people and then transporting them from one site to another. They knew the drill, and they worked with each other seamlessly. A quiet word from Marla, and a certain group of dogs went into one van and another into a closed truck. Each vehicle was loaded and moved into the line.

The drivers then helped with the next load or drank hot coffee from old thermoses and talked in gentle voices to each other. Additional empty crates and supplies went into the back of the rental truck. The last crate fit in the back of Marla's van. She moved them into place, and loaded them with the mother dog and puppies. As the light came to the sky, the caravan moved out of the yard. Kat drew maps and written instructions. Peter handed each driver an envelope with a copy of the map, the instructions, and cash for round-trip ferry fare. The fare was welcome but unnecessary; dog people helped other dog people, even if they couldn't afford it.

Kat asked Clair if she could hire her to provide food for the move day. Clair was happy to help. She and Kat planned the menu for the day and went food shopping on Friday after the bakery closed. Kat paid for the food, but Clair refused to accept money from her friend for her time and labor.

Clair dropped Kat off and drove home to unload the supplies. The phoned was ringing as she walked in the door.

"Clair, I know you are probably going to bite me, but I think we should add roast beef sandwiches. I mean, what if some people don't like pasta salad? Not that your chicken pasta salad isn't wonderful, because it is." Kat spoke in a rushed, pressured manner. Clair had never heard her like that before. It was also totally out of character for Kat to obsess about food.

"OK—" Clair started to answer, but Kat interrupted her.

"I am so sorry; I am not usually so indecisive. I mean, I used to be, but I just want everything to be perfect tomorrow—and I can go back to town and pick up the roasts if you tell me exactly what to buy."

Clair could feel Kat's tension running through the phone line.

"Kat, it isn't a problem. They're easy to make. I'll call Mom and ask her to pick up the meat and some french bread on her way up."

"Oh, that would be great. Do you think she would mind? Do you want me to call her?"

"Kat, breathe. This is not a big deal. We can handle it."

Just as Clair hung up the phone, Molly burst through the dog door. The black, wet, sandy dog ran circles around her as she made the call to her mother.

Fortunately, Tasha was already planning to come up for the weekend. She was in the ferry line when Clair reached her. Clair was pleasantly surprised when her mother did not comment on or try to alter the menu in any way. And she agreed to stop and pick up the beef roasts and french bread on her way up the island.

Friday night, they baked the cookies, roasted the beef, and poached the chicken for the salad. Clair grudgingly admitted, if only to herself, that after a week in the bakery, she was grateful to see her mother. And they actually worked together compatibly in the kitchen.

Clair was in the new Bird Farm kitchen very early on Saturday morning making potato soup and baking monkey bread. There would also be chicken pasta salad, chocolate chip cookies, and, of course, the roast beef sandwiches.

Mike Bell and one of his crews also arrived early to work on the medium-sized outbuilding that was being remodeled for mother dogs and their puppies. Molly and Cerberus were checking out the large fenced area, which lay directly off of the main kennel building.

Kat was setting up a buffet table. It was way too early to expect the vans, but she found herself looking out the front window every few minutes. She tried to help Clair, but she was basically useless in the kitchen. Tasha arrived with the chicken pasta salad that she'd already put together, assessed the situation, and asked Clair, "Do you want me to slice the roasts?"

I looked at the clock on the kitchen wall. It read 12:00. No, that couldn't be right. The treacherous thing was showing the correct time when I arrived earlier.

I ignored the clock with the resigned sigh of a time-challenged person and answered my mother, "Sure, Mom, that would be good. What time is it?"

Kat was pacing from the kitchen to the living room window and back again. This was a problem because part of the living room was blocked off for a mother dog and her puppies. Every time she walked through the area, the puppies became semiwild. She answered over a cacophony of puppy barks.

"It's about ten o'clock."

"What time are you expecting them?" Tasha asked as she finished slicing the second roast and began arranging a vegetable platter.

"Marla said about noon," Kat answered, almost tripping Clair, who was backing away from the oven with two hot Bundt pans of monkey bread.

Tasha noticed that there was a bakery box full of cinnamon rolls. She quickly made another pot of coffee and sent Kat out to the crew with a tray of coffee and cinnamon rolls. After serving the grateful work crew, Kat walked through the main kennel building, checking again that each separate room had a dog bed and a full bowl of clean water. The weather was cool and misty, but it looked like the rain might hold off for the day. Kat took that as a very positive sign.

The first van arrived at 11:30 a.m., and by noon the yard was full of vehicles, dogs, and people. Getting the dogs settled in their new home was the first priority. Marla and Kat already decided where each dog would be housed. Each kennel room was labeled and new beds were put in with fleece covers. Each newly arrived group of dogs was allowed to run free in the exercise area and then shifted to their assigned kennel. This took over an hour.

The two mother dogs with litters would be kept in the house until the remodeling on the nursery was completed. Athena's pups were weaned and had their own quarters. The large sunlit living room was given over to nursery purposes without a second thought. When the dogs were settled to Marla's satisfaction, the people could be fed. The house was full and alive with people and dogs. The work crew was invited to join the group for lunch, and Clair and Tasha were busy keeping the buffet table replenished with food. By 2:00

Mike's crew was back at work, and by 2:30 the volunteer drivers were ready to head back to the peninsula. Tasha had already stared to clean up the kitchen. Peter and Josh unloaded Marla's furniture while Kat and Marla checked on the dogs.

I needed to get out of the kitchen. Tasha was reloading the dishwasher.

"I'm going to take a break," I said over my shoulder as I hastily left the kitchen.

"Good," Tasha responded, "we're almost finished here."

I went upstairs to see how Marla's stuff was working out in the bedrooms.

Peter was just starting down the stairs, and we met in the middle.

"The food was great. Thank you for helping my sister. I know she's hopeless with food," Peter said, placing a light hand on my shoulder.

"Kat is a good friend. I'm happy to help her."

"Damn. I was hoping you did it to impress me," Peter said with a chuckle, putting his other hand on my other shoulder.

"Not likely. Although I may have a few impressions to correct with you."

"I'm not sure exactly what you mean by that."

"I don't like looking up at you," I said abruptly.

"Well, we can fix that." Peter took my hand and led me to the top of the stairs. He again put a light hand on each of my shoulders, as if to hold me in place, and moved around to stand on the step below me. "How is this?" he asked. We were almost at an equal height now. He dropped his hands from my shoulders and brought one up to cup my face with it. He placed his other hand gently on my waist. I considered two conflicting courses of action: I wanted to kiss Peter. His lips were perfectly on my level. And I wanted to turn and run.

Peter rubbed his thumb over my cheek and then softly over my lips. He moved closer to kiss me, and I met him half-way. No thinking was involved, and I felt all the tension melt out of my body. I sighed softly, leaning in for another kiss.

Loud footsteps sounded across the hallway behind us.

"Blocking the exit from the second floor is considered a grave security breach," Josh said. "At least let me get around you. I don't like being trapped up here, especially when there's ongoing action at the exit point."

Peter groaned, acknowledging that the mood was broken. He saluted Josh, smiled at Clair, and turned around to move down the stairs. Suddenly, he changed his mind and detoured around Josh to follow Clair up to the second floor.

Josh smiled to himself as he left Peter and Clair. He planned to check the ground floor windows again, but he heard Tasha in the kitchen. He decided that he was desperate for more chocolate chip cookies. Tasha knew he was in the kitchen before she turned around.

"I need some more of those chocolate chip cookies."

"I don't think so," Tasha replied.

Josh threw her a wolfish grin. "You are correct. It was a completely fabricated reason to seek you out." He moved toward her.

Tasha thought back to New Year's Eve in her kitchen.

"Do you think it's significant that we frequently meet in kitchens?"

"You make me hungry?" Josh suggested as he placed his hands on the kitchen counter on either side of Tasha.

Josh's arms trapped Tasha, but she didn't feel trapped.

"No, I think you are always hungry…Josh." She made no move to escape the circle of his arms. The sound of his name slowed him down.

"Are we back to the predator and prey routine?"

"No, I refuse to be anyone's prey anymore…I did tell you that," Tasha responded seriously.

"Well, I don't want a bite—I just want a taste." He surprised them both by leaning in and gently brushing his mouth across hers.

The evening found the move completed and everyone exhausted. A second bedroom was set up for Kat, who wanted to spend the first night at the kennel house. Josh explained the alarm system twice. He turned on the floodlights around the outside kennel areas and then left for the beach house with Peter. They planned to stay on the island for the rest of the weekend. Clair, Tasha, and Molly departed for home. The dogs and people settled in for the night.

Josh and Peter were enjoying beer and leftovers at the beach house. The fog moved in close around the house. They were sitting in the living room in front of a comforting fire. Josh picked up the local weekly paper and was reading it while he ate.

"Damn." Peter was surprised by Josh's outburst.

"What?"

"Someone stole a dumpster."

"That doesn't sound so terrible," Peter responded.

"It's an indicator. There haven't been any more incidents since the fall. Now there's this."

"That doesn't seem like a big deal, Josh."

"By itself, it isn't, but it was stolen from the dump in this area, and it may be part of the pattern that started in the fall. I think I'll stay on the island until my team gets the security system installed on the outbuildings."

CHAPTER 22

FEBRUARY AT THE BAKERY was steady, but it seemed slow after the whirlwind of the holidays. Clair was happy to help Katelyn with food for the moving day. Her friendship with her beach neighbor was growing, and she hoped that the opening of the kennel would not bring an end to that.

"What are we gonna do about Sadie?" Tina asked Clair as they were cleaning up after Friday lunch at the bakery.

"I don't know. Part of me says we don't have to and shouldn't do anything. Sadie is her own person and makes her own decisions about her life," I replied.

"She's got no family around here, so we are her family. You know she's gotten to a place where she needs more help than we can give her," Tina pointed out.

I sighed. I knew that Tina was right, but I dreaded talking to Sadie again about more help.

"She also needs to give up another day here."

"I know. She's so tired by Thursday afternoon that I'm

afraid she is going to collapse. But, Tina, it's her decision, and it is not as if we haven't pointed out the possibilities to her."

"When that basset hound pulls her down and she breaks her hip, or when she burns the house down because she forgot the soup on the stove, how will we feel?"

"You're right, of course. I will talk to her again. Kat's thinking of hiring a high school student to help with the kennel after school and on the weekends. Maybe if that works out, we could get the same person or one of her friends to walk Sophie."

"Sadie needs a housekeeper *and* a dog walker," Tina grumbled.

I dropped in on Saturday with sandwiches and soup to check on Sadie. I knocked on the back door and came in through the kitchen. Sophie tried to trip me, but I was ready for the hound. It took all of my courage to talk to Sadie, and I was not one bit closer to getting more help for my old friend and boss when I left.

Damn, he hated this island. Nothing worked out the way he planned. The bird farm property wasn't supposed to sell. He was so sure that he set the price high enough to keep it on the market for at least a year. He worked hard to set himself up as a real estate agent in the state. He talked that secretary into getting him the state listing, wined and dined the stupid bitch until she gave him what he wanted. He wanted to use her longer, pump her for information about other state land available before it was announced to the general public, but she was getting suspicious. She would keep her mouth shut because, as he explained to her, legally, she was the guilty party. What the hell was wrong with these people? No one would sell his or her piece-of-crap house. He nearly had the loan lined up, but he needed a big block of land. Well, he would just have to increase the pressure. He knew how to do that.

"Hey, babe, you are looking so smart today. Damn, gorgeous, when are you gonna go out with me?" He slid in next to a plain-looking, middle-aged woman. He made it a point to have lunch in the cafeteria of the Hospital Corporation dining room once a week, never on the same day. A small bribe to the security guard gave him free access to the secretary of the corporation's vice president who was in charge of acquisitions and mergers.

⁓

As the year moved into March, the island remained cocooned in a cold, wet mist. The bakery's special offerings were shamrock cookies and Reuben sandwiches for Friday lunches. My friend Shannon and I sat at table four. It was Friday afternoon, and the lunch hour was officially over. The bakery was cleaned and closed. Tina just left with the week's leftovers to be delivered. Shannon called me earlier. "Hey, I haven't seen you, forever."

"I know. Between the bakery and the kennel opening, I've been almost under water. Are you off this afternoon? Can you come over for a late lunch?"

"I'm on night shift, so it's a possibility. What's for lunch?"

"I'll save us some Reuben sandwiches."

"Great, see you at about three o'clock."

I was excited to see Shannon, both to catch up on her life and to see if she had any input into possible living situations for Sadie.

"These sandwiches are great!" Shannon exclaimed.

"Thanks, they've been a big hit," I said, smiling brightly. "Shannon, are there any independent or assisted-living facilities on the island?"

"There are very few. We have a couple of nursing homes and a few private rooms in people's homes. Only one of the nursing homes has rehab abilities. It's a big problem. The discharge planner at the hospital has a terrible time placing people who need that kind of care. Mostly, they have to go off the island."

"That is so strange since the island seems to be a retirement mecca."

"Yeah, it's the reason the hospital was able to expand last year. They actually considered adding an extended-care wing. But they decided to just add a rehab department. Are you thinking about Sadie?"

As usual, Shannon went right to the heart of my questions.

"Yes, it's getting harder and harder for her. Tina and I have tried to get her help, but she's so stubborn."

"If Sadie needs to have extended care, it'll be difficult to find it on the island. Although, there *is* a rumor that Hospital Corporation is considering a large progressive-care facility here."

"I am so worried about her. Mom says we need to be ready with alternatives when the crisis comes. I don't want it to come to a crisis."

"I hate to be so negative, but your mother is probably right."

"I hate to have you agree with my mother. Hey, how about some shamrock cookies for dessert?"

"Yum. How about going out with Nick and me tomorrow night? Tyree Tavern has live music."

"Can't. I promised to help Kat at the kennel."

They both knew it was a total or partial fabrication, and they both accepted it. Shannon developed her patience though her nursing. She would not give up on her friend.

Sadie found herself online again. She knew that her book buying was becoming an obsession. She told herself she could stop when she just found the perfect book, the book that gave her the wisdom that she needed. She spent hours researching her selections, reading their synopses and reviews. She bought in two categories: wisdom and escape. She knew that if she could just collect enough knowledge and find a way to apply it, she would be content. She was fiercely independent and wanted to stay that way until the end. She wasn't afraid of death, but she admitted, if only to herself, that she might still fear the manner of her death—not the death, but the dying. She resisted all her daughter's offers to relocate closer to her. For escape, lately, she was reading children's literature.

The good feelings that she got when she selected a book and ordered it didn't last. She couldn't even remember what she had ordered the next day. There were piles of unopened book boxes in her house. Sometimes it made her feel safe to have so many books around her, so many possibilities. Sometimes it overwhelmed her. She collected books like she used to collect recipes. She was moving away from that part of her life. She had lost interest in the bakery. She continued to bake because it gave her income, and income meant independence. If she was honest with herself, and she always was, she liked being with Clair and Tina. Baking gave her a reason to get up in the morning and get out of the house. It was something she did well. She didn't have to think about it. But saying she was tired didn't even begin to cover the way she felt.

The bakery offerings for April were all about spring. But the weather did not corroborate the time of year. Work on the Bird Farm Kennels progressed; the construction team worked on the fencing and outbuildings as the weather permitted and on the inside areas when it did not. They were almost done with the building designated for the nursing dogs and their puppies. Peter found himself on the island most weekends. Josh set up a temporary security system for the outside areas. He was also spending most of his weekends on the island.

CHAPTER 23

"CHIEF SNAKELUM'S GRAVE GETS a Facelift," the title read.

The picture showed a standard gray gravestone in the middle of a densely wooded area. Luke read the article with interest. But the comments were political, and the research regarding the chief's life, death, and genuine resting place was nonexistent. He couldn't tell from the picture if it was the same place he visited with Kat and Clair months before. Maybe it was time for another visit to the island. The thought made him smile. He would give Tasha a call and see if she wanted to go.

They found the grave easily. It was right where Luke remembered it. But now, in place of the dirt mound, the rocks, and the seashells, there was a generic concrete gravestone with the chief's name and the supposed dates of his birth and death.

"Not very authentic," Tasha commented.

"Not as bad as it could be. It was a political gesture from the governor to the Indian tribes of the state."

"Well, I believe that she missed the mark," Tasha answered as she walked around the gravesite.

"A total miss," Luke agreed.

"Although," she paused and took a deep breath, "the area does have a stillness…it feels peaceful."

"Yes, I felt that the first time we found the spot. I am glad you can still feel it."

After the gravesite visit, Tasha suggested that they stop at the kennel. Luke agreed, and they spent an agreeable afternoon with Kat, Marla, and a dog cast of mass proportions. Kat was excited to share the progress with them. She suggested they stay for dinner and even overnight. "Peter and Josh will be here for the weekend."

"I would love to, but I've got to study for midterms," Tasha responded.

"I haven't made any arrangements for Isis or the museum," Luke said.

"Isis is Luke's Siamese cat," Tasha clarified.

"I remember," Kat said.

Kat looked so sad that Tasha added, "I'm coming up in two weeks for spring break. Maybe Luke will come too."

Two pairs of female eyes turned toward Luke.

"Please come. I'm sure Peter and Josh will be here," pleaded Kat. "We'll have such a good time! I'm spending most of my time here, but there is plenty of room at the beach house."

Luke looked uncertain. Tasha winked at Kat. "I'll work

on him."

Nothing ever went the way he planned it. "My life sucks," he said, clenching his fists.

His old man finally came through with the job he had been promising for months. But that was f—d. He was supposed to be driving the garbage truck. But because he didn't have his f—ing high school certification, his job was picking up road kill off the highway. Just great! He hated his life, but at least he found a way to make some money. He loved dumping garbage in the old lady's yard. He and his buddy Travis almost lost it spray painting her roof. The damn thing was slanted and slick as snot. But they'd done that well. And now they had another job.

"Peter…Saint Peter, best of brothers. Are you coming up this weekend?" Kat's voice on the phone was as excited as it was pleading.

"Well, I guess so. I hadn't really gotten to the weekend plans yet…but I'm slightly apprehensive about your eagerness to have me. What wild scheme do you want to involve me in?"

"Snoqualmie just won best in class. That means she will be showing in best of show on the weekend. I really want to be there. It would only be one night."

"Slow down, Kat. I'm lost. Is Snoqualmie one of the

dogs?"

"Yes, Marla is showing her and a few of the others at the Pacific Northwest Dog Show this week."

"You mean you've been alone at the kennel all week?" Peter felt his heart begin to pound in his chest.

"Don't worry. Josh knows about it."

"He knew about it and didn't tell me? I'll wring his neck!"

"Peter, don't. I swore him to secrecy. He calls to check on me almost every hour, brings me lunch every day, and comes up at night to help with the dogs and set up the security systems."

"How long has this been going on?"

"Only three days. Peter, what I need is for you to be at the kennel Saturday and Saturday night so I can go to the show. It's so important to me." His sister went on about the dog's bloodlines, the breeding programs, the future of the kennel—he tuned it all out.

"I knew I should have insisted on a kennel manager before this."

"We'll get one. It hasn't been a problem up to now. I just really want to there for this show."

"Kat, I know nothing about running a kennel."

"Come up on Friday, and I'll teach you. Peter, please. I promise that Marla and I will start looking for a kennel manager next week."

Peter pulled up his appointment calendar and let out a big sigh. "I'll be up there late Thursday night."

Peter immediately called Josh.

"*Merde*!" Josh identified Peter as the caller.

"What the hell—" Peter started

Josh interrupted him. "I have her on a continuous monitor feed all day. And I've slept in my car outside the house every damn night."

"In the Jag?"

"For the first night. Then I rented a bigger car," Josh admitted.

Peter let out a breath he didn't realize he had been holding. He pictured Josh spending the night in his car. "I don't think I am paying you enough."

"Damn right about that. She didn't tell me Marla was going to be gone until after Marla left, and she swore me secrecy. How does she do that?"

"I don't know. But she just got me to agree to run the kennel this weekend so that she can go to the dog show," Peter admitted.

Josh laughed. "I'll see you on Thursday."

Peter caught the last ferry to the island on Thursday night. He and Kat spent Friday going over the kennel routine. Kat typed up a working schedule for him, and he took notes on a clipboard. Josh brought over halibut and chips for dinner.

"At least I'll get to sleep in a bed tonight," Josh said when Kat was out of the room.

"Show me again how to set the system before you leave," Peter said.

Kat and Cerberus were set to catch the first ferry on Saturday morning. They left before it was light. Peter was feeling very sorry for himself as he drank a second cup of coffee. He rummaged through the kitchen cupboards and looked in the refrigerator. "Damn, what does she live on?" He made himself wait until 6:00 a.m. and then called Josh. "Help. There's no human food in this place. I need you to go on a supply run for me."

He wanted to call Clair, but it was way too early for that. Josh showed up about 9:30 a.m. with groceries. He stashed them in the kitchen and checked on Peter.

He was feeding the late eaters. Some of the dogs ate early and then there was the latter group.

Peter didn't want to do the two puppy rooms. It was a real adventure to get them all outside at one time and get their area cleaned. He had just started to spray down one of the rooms when two of the puppies ran back inside. They thought that the hose was a great game. Peter dropped the hose to chase them out. He was sure he clicked the sprayer to the off position.

The hose had a powerful spray attachment, and Peter did not expect the force of the water. He was soaked.

Kat was well organized. There was a large notebook in the central kennel area that had a section for each dog. The type and amount of food for each dog was listed, as well as their feeding times. The food containers were labeled so the job seemed straightforward. But by the time Josh came to find him, Peter was tired and wet. Each kennel space had to be sprayed clean while the dogs were in the exercise area. That meant taking out the beds first. Not all the dogs were friends, so he had to let them out in agreeable groups. As a result, he had to check his clipboard frequently. He didn't know the dogs, and they refused to tell him their names, so he had to continually refer to the names outside each kennel room. Some of the dogs didn't want to go back into their rooms after their allotted time outside. Peter found himself trying to persuade Minerva to go back into her room.

When Josh arrived, he saw a dirty and damp man talking earnestly to a large Doberman pincher, who was pointedly ignoring him.

Josh stepped into the yard, snapped a leash on the bitch, and she walked, calmly and agreeably at his side, to her room. He looked at Peter and raised one of his eyebrows. "Did Zeus spill his water again?"

"No, it just took me a little time to get the hose routine down. Wait, you know their names?"

"Naturally," Josh answered.

Peter looked so exhausted that Josh almost felt sorry for him.

"It takes a while. I brought sustenance. Come on, take a break."

They headed back to the house. Peter looked down at his jeans.

"It was the puppies," he mumbled.

Josh smiled. "Yeah, they are little devils, aren't they?"

"I don't understand. I've never had trouble with dogs before. I swear, these dogs are laughing at me."

"What? Didn't you tell them that you have an MBA and managed a multimillion-dollar corporation?"

"Please, Clair. I am desperate."

"OK, but I get to pick the movie."

Clair arrived at the Bird Farm Kennels with a pizza, a DVD, and assorted supplies to get them both through the night. Fortunately, Molly was spending the night with Tasha. One more dog would probably not be a good thing. Peter had not finished the evening exercise and feeding routine. He met her at the car door.

"Thank you for coming."

Clair had never seen Peter so disheveled. Even at his most casual, there was always a polished aura around him—but not tonight.

"Have you finished the evening schedule?"

"Ah…no. Do you want to help?" he asked hopefully.

I laughed.

"Peter Cameron, you lured me here under false pretenses. I thought I was getting a night of pizza, a movie, and free sex, but I find that I'm expected to slave in the dog trenches."

"No, no, you don't have to help," he answered quickly.

"It's all right. I won't abandon you, and I like working with the dogs."

"You do? What about the puppies?" Peter asked hopefully.

"I love the puppies. They're so much fun."

"You do? They are? They terrify me."

I could not imagine anything terrifying Peter.

We dropped off the people supplies in the house and headed for the kennels. We spent an hour playing with the two sets of puppies. By the time we were ready to leave the nursery and move on to the remaining adult dogs, Peter was relaxed and smiling. I fixed a picture in my mind of Peter lying on the grass and letting six puppies crawl all over him. He wrestled gently with the older ones, threw small balls, and played tug and chase. The next hour went smoothly, and by 7:30 p.m., all the dogs had run, played, and eaten. All were in their rooms for the night.

Peter put his arm around me as we walked to the house.

"I hesitate to mention this, but do I detect a slight odor of dog?" I asked playfully.

Peter learned down to kiss me. "You are right, a distinct doggie scent. I'll meet you in the shower." And he did.

The living room was full of dog crates. Until recently, it was a home for the nursing puppies and their mothers. Eventually, it would be furnished, but Kat and Marla did not consider it a priority at that time. Peter and Clair took their pizza and DVD to Kat's bedroom. It had a flat-screen TV with DVD player and a queen-size bed.

"I'm afraid to ask what movie you selected," Peter said.

"French with subtitles," I answered.

Peter groaned.

"What? Do my ears deceive me? I did my doggie duty, and you'll keep your part of the bargain."

They watched *Queen to Play* and snuggled together on Kat's bed with a bulldog named Quincy. Quincy and Cerberus were the only house dogs. All the dogs spent time inside the house. Marla was adamant about socialization for all the Dobermans. But the house dogs were those that lived and slept in the house. Cerberus was Kat's companion and accompanied her to the dog show.

Quincy established himself on the bed between Peter and Clair. He scored several large bites of pizza and now snored loudly and contentedly, with only occasional bouts of gas, through the end of the movie. Even in his sleep, he resisted being moved.

"What do you know about this guy?"

"Kat told me that Quincy was given to Marla by a friend who breeds bulldogs when she lost her last house dog. He is quite a character, isn't he?"

"That he is," Peter answered as he scratched behind the bulldog's ears. "Are we going to have to spend the whole night with him?"

"No," I answered with a smile. "He is very well behaved for a bulldog. We'll need to take him out one more time. Then I think he will sleep on Marla's bed. What did you think of the movie?"

"Well, it was definitely a woman's movie."

"*Mais, bein sur* (but of course)," I answered

"It didn't portray men in a very favorable manner."

"No, but I don't think that was the primary intent. The gender issues were certainly there, but I think it was about being brave and taking risks. I think the whole point of the movie was when he said to her, 'If you take a risk, there is a *chance* you will lose. If you don't take the risk, you *will* lose.'"

"Maybe that is more of a woman's issue. In business, you learn to take risks."

"I'm not a risk taker," I said, rather sadly.

"To be an effective risk taker, you have to know what you want," Peter answered.

"I want time to stop moving, to just be still until I can grasp who and what I am and where I need to go."

"And yet, you are obsessed with time. I've observed that even though clocks and watches aren't accurate around you, you always know what time it is.

"Yes, I am endlessly aware of time passing, moving, eluding me."

"Are you equating time to life?"

"Well, time is life."

"No, Clair. Time is a made-up measurement. Einstein said time doesn't exist."

"Maybe I just don't know what I want."

"And what are you doing to try to find out?"

"I guess I am finding out by default, weeding out what I don't want. I thought I wanted to do pure research. At first the university seemed so safe. The history department was an entity unto itself, and I was a part of it. But I hated the backstabbing when I came to understand how competitive and political it was—even among those of us who didn't teach. I thought we would be immune. We had no interest in professorships or tenure. But then it was all about who you worked for and what kind of status your professor had in the history department, as if the person you worked for gave you some kind of vicarious glory. It was very intense and very unhealthy."

"So you quit and came to the island. That was a risk, Clair. I think you're braver than you think."

"Well," I said in a lighter tone, "the timing gods are smiling on me, and I do know what I want to do tonight."

"I hope that means spending the night with me."

"It does, but it does *not* involve sleeping with this loudly snoring bulldog."

"OK, let's risk waking the sleeping beast."

We woke and walked Quincy, then transferred him to Marla's bed for the night.

I woke up slowly, feeling amazingly rested and content. I felt Peter's large, warm body next to me, and I thought about snuggling closer to him until I saw the clock on the dresser.

"Oh, I'm late. I'm so late."

"Oh, my dear whiskers, oh my dear fur, have you turned into Alice's white rabbit?" Peter teased, throwing an arm around me and pulling me close for a kiss.

"Peter, it's late!"

"Yes, Clair it's late, but the world did not stop turning, and the sun is still in the sky. And it's Sunday, so relax a little. I, however, may be in serious trouble. It's past feeding time, and those puppies are going to eat me alive. Do you think your timing issue is contagious?"

CHAPTER 24

MIDTERMS WERE OVER AND her master's thesis was on schedule.

Tasha was on spring break and planning to spend at least a week on the island. Luke accepted Kat's invite and was also coming up to spend a few days. They were driving up together but in separate cars. Tasha was uncertain when she would return, and Luke was equally unsure about the length of his stay. As she sat in the ferry line, Tasha thought back to the last time she was with Josh. She needed to get her feelings about this man clear. She knew he was staying at Kat's beach house. It was one of the reasons Luke agreed to go. He liked Josh and felt comfortable with him.

Josh called her a week after the great kennel move in. He told her he was in Seattle on business for the day and asked if she wanted to go to dinner with him. They agreed to meet at a Chinese restaurant in the University District. Tasha thought she needed neutral territory. She acknowledged that there was an electric attraction between the two of them. They had been playing touch and retreat since they met. They were both reluctant to turn it into a relationship. Tasha was sure that she didn't want to deal with a man, any man, right now—at least not on a serious level. She needed to use all her energy to reach the goal she set for herself. Clair would understand. She felt that she had limited time and funding to achieve that goal. She could not, would not, allow herself to be distracted. But when she was with Josh, he didn't seem like a distraction. He felt like part of a whole.

He was waiting for her outside the restaurant. He kissed her on the cheek and guided her to a table he had preselected and reserved. It was at the back of the room and had a good view of both the entry and the kitchen door. The food was great. They talked about the kennel and their mutual friends. They talked about Paris. They talked about Josh's security business and Tasha's master thesis. It was a pleasant and comfortable evening. They touched each other easily, as if they had been partners for a long time. She reached for the teapot and their hands brushed as he reached for a serving dish. His knee touched hers under the table.

The meal was finished, and the tension began to build between them. Tasha refilled their cup with the jasmine tea she loved. Josh's cup was still half full.

"I don't need a man to complete me," she blurted out.

Josh raised his eyebrows.

"Acknowledged," he said.

"Acknowledged?" she questioned.

"Yes, I acknowledged the fact that you don't need a man

to make you a complete human being."

"But? I sense a 'but.'"

"It seems important for you to clarify the boundaries of our relationship. But I think that the lady doth protest too much."

"Meaning?"

"Meaning that *I* don't need to be anyone's reason for existence."

"Ah," Tasha breathed.

"Ah?" Josh asked.

"I think we may both have been on other sides of this equation in our past lives."

"So where does that leave us now?"

"Sadder but wiser."

"But doesn't wisdom bring with it a clearer path?"

Tasha thought for a moment. "Sometimes, but I am not feeling all that clear tonight."

"Lady, I would truly love to sleep with you, but you may be more than I can handle."

"I don't think there is much you can't handle," she quipped back.

"Tasha, I don't *need* sex from you, but I *want* it. I am not into relationship drama. I don't have a problem being your friend *and* your lover."

And he proved it, she remembered. He was a superb lover, and he left the next morning as a friend. He called her a few times since then, but they had not been together. She would see him in a few hours. He offered to rent a room or a cabin, if he could find one, for the week. She still wasn't sure if she wanted that and didn't push it. She was almost there now. What the hell was she going to do?

"Hey, I think this line stretches to Alaska. Do you want to get some clam strips?" Luke asked, knocking on her window. Tasha shook herself out of her memories and saw that they would have at least a two-ferry wait. She and Luke locked their cars and walked to Ivor's takeout window on the ferry dock. It was late evening when they finally arrived at Kat's beach house. Tasha decided to see Josh before she went to see Clair. But Josh, it turned out, was at the kennels checking security for the night. "He checks it almost every night," Kat told her. "He is almost as protective as my brother."

Josh finished his tour of the Bird Farm property, checked and rechecked the systems, and said good night to Marla. Everything was working, but Josh's gut was telling him to be on alert, and that was one system he learned not to ignore. He turned his old green Jaguar down the road toward Kat's beach house but changed his mind. The missed message on his cell was Kat asking him to join her at Tyree, the one and only local bar. They did not serve food. They served beer, alcohol, and, occasionally, live music.

The bar was dark and full of people. A very small country music band was leaving the makeshift stage at one end of the room, and several couples were exiting the dance floor. All the tables looked full. Josh paid the cover charge and stood by the door until he had a clear picture of the dim interior.

Tasha moved out of a booth in the back of the room. She spoke briefly to a man at the bar. He nodded. She picked up his guitar and stepped up onto the stage. There was movement at side of the stage, which turned out to be Clair. She was pressing buttons on a karaoke machine. Some introductory music responded to her machinations, but Tasha didn't need it. She played the introduction on the borrowed guitar. Josh moved closer as she began to sing.

"God, I feel like hell tonight."

The lights came up on her, and the karaoke machine provided additional backup music. Josh vaguely recognized the Sheryl Crow song. He faced Tasha across the dance floor, and she sang directly to him. Time was suspended.

"Are you strong enough to be my man?" she sang.

The bar exploded with applause.

"More!" Whistle. Claps. "Encore!"

"No, no." Tasha shook her head and left the stage.

She stopped in front of Josh and mumbled, "I'm a one-trick pony. It's the only song I can play…" she trailed off and shook her head slightly, as if to clear it. She walked quickly to a booth where Kat and Luke were sitting. She reached in a grabbed her purse and her coat. She muttered something about needing some air and headed for the exit.

Her performance had energized the crowd. Peter moved up next to Clair, who was still at the machine. Nick was pulling Shannon onstage, and the Journey song "Any Way You Want It" filled the room.

Josh followed Tasha out the door and around to the side of the building. The parking lot was full, but no one was around.

Tasha knew that Josh was behind her. She didn't know what she wanted to do about it. She just realized that her car was not in the lot. She rode to the tavern with Kat and Luke, and she didn't have a way home. Not only had she broken one of her own ironclad rules—*always drive yourself, always have a way out*—she had made a spectacle of herself, drawn attention to herself. Her actions were so out of character. She was shaken by her own behavior. She was also vulnerable. That was something she could not, would not, allow. She took a deep breath, slipped back into character, and flashed Josh a seductive smile.

"Well, *are* you strong enough to be *my* man?"

Josh moved closer to her but didn't touch her, which slightly defused the sexually charged atmosphere. "That was a class act."

"Act is exactly what it was. It's what I am always doing. Tasha the role player, wife, mother, nurse, student, would-be counselor—"

"Gypsy?" offered Josh, leaning even closer.

"Gypsy," she agreed with a lowered head.

A tear ran down her cheek. "I am so afraid that I will run out of roles," she said in a choked voice.

Josh circled her with his arms and pulled her to him. He held her gently and let her cry.

"I understand role playing." He murmured into her hair.

A timeless moment later, Tasha raised her head.

"I am so sorry. I didn't mean to dissolve on you." She sniffed slightly. "Please forgive me."

Josh dropped his arms. "Consider yourself forgiven."

"Would you please drive me home?"

"Absolutely."

Tasha was silent on the ride to the beach, but when Josh pulled to a stop on the road behind the beach house, she spoke as if continuing a conversation.

"I'm not altogether opposed to a little casual sex. In fact, I've become a rather recent advocate."

Josh raised both eyebrows slightly. "Strange. When you are not in your gypsy mode, I don't see you as a proponent of casual sex."

"Making up for lost opportunities," she answered in a low voice.

"Well then, by all means, allow me to assist you in any way possible."

"No."

"No?"

"I just can't see you as a casual acquaintance."

"Oh, I can be very casual," he assured her with a lazy smile.

"Not for me."

"Tasha, opportunities lost are opportunities gone. You can't make up for them."

"See what I mean? You are not as casual as you pretend to be," she pointed out.

He let the silence settle between them.

"I'll be ready in half an hour," she said, bolting out of the car.

"I'll be back to pick you up in twenty-five minutes."

Tasha let Molly out for a short run on the beach and

scribbled a note to Clair.

"Going home for the night. Call you later."

Josh threw together an overnight bag and left a brief note for Peter.

"On night maneuvers—systems working at the kennels. Back tomorrow."

Tasha was waiting for him.

"How do you feel about the Captain Whidbey Inn?" Josh asked.

Tasha laughed. "It's the perfect place for a pirate encounter."

The night was long. *Another piece of time suspended, out of the context of my life*, Tasha thought as she woke late in the morning. Josh was not in the bed, but she knew that he hadn't left. She took her time in the shower. It was almost noon by the time she left the room. She found Josh in the inn's dining room. He was standing at the window, looking out at the inlet of the bay.

"Hi, want some lunch?" he asked.

"Lunch would be great. Suddenly, I am ravenous."

Josh laughed as he steered her to a corner table. "I think you are a lady of healthy appetites."

Tasha thought about that for a moment. "You know, I am. And recently, I have become braver about expressing those appetites."

"I like my women strong."

I know you do—so they won't fall apart when you leave them, Tasha thought but didn't say out loud. Instead, she said, "*My* women?"

"Oh no. Now I am going to get the male-chauvinist-pig lecture."

Tasha looked at him, considering. "No, I think the recognition of sin will suffice."

"Does that mean that I have possibilities?"

"I am sure you have possibilities, Josh, but not with me."

The waitress brought their drinks and took their lunch order.

"I don't see you as a male hater."

"I'm not. Not anymore. I just think we are on different paths."

"You mean, 'I'm Not Talking about Forever.'"

Tasha laughed. "Ah, are you proposing a kind of Toby Keith meets Sheryl Crow for the night?"

Josh smiled at her. "Well, I guess I think of myself as more of a Bruce Springsteen type. Occasionally, I need a little 'Human Touch.' But I wasn't actually proposing anything, more hypothesizing."

"Of course not. Cowboys like to think they are spontaneous, no preplanning that might lead to afterthoughts. Cowboys are action figures." Tasha responded

Josh choked on his beer. Tasha looked over at him.

"What, not a cowboy?" she asked tauntingly.

"Hell no. Not now." And then, reflectively, he said, "Well, I may have been a cowboy once or twice in my past life."

A laugh broke from Tasha. "Yes, definitely a possibility."

"Cowboy. Action figure. Pirate. You know, for someone who's trying to escape being typecast into roles herself, you sure can label."

"Touché, well done. I think we should just leave it at a draw. I am suddenly tired."

"The action figure in me says that is exactly the time to press forward."

"You mean attack?"

"I deliberately didn't use that word."

"Ah, a thinking cowboy. Very frightening."

"You mean very threatening?"

"Back off, action figure. I am damaged, and I haven't finished remaking myself yet," Tasha snarled.

"We are all damaged, Tasha. We're human, but we're still alive," Josh answered in a gentle voice.

They ordered lunch and ate it in companionable silence. Despite the recent subject matter, there was no tension between them.

"I think we should move in together," Josh blurted out. "I can't believe I said that."

"Why? Because it gives me too much power in the relationship?"

"Hell, I'm not even willing to concede that we have a relationship."

Tasha laughed lightly.

"You can relax. I don't want us to live together."

"You don't?"

"No. I am not sure what I do want us to do together, but I am certain that I don't want us to cohabitate. And I agree that we probably don't have a long-term relationship."

Josh took an audibly deep breath. He walked around the table and pulled out her chair. As they walked out of the restaurant, he put his arm around her shoulder and pulled her next to him.

"OK, gypsy girl. We will just take it day to day for a little longer."

CHAPTER 25

ON TUESDAY MORNING, CLAIR stopped to pick up Sadie. Her boss was usually waiting on her front porch, but there was no sign of her outside the house that morning. It was cold and damp, so Clair was not terribly alarmed. She also checked in with Sadie last night. The old woman was settled in bed early with a cup of tea, Sophie, and a book when she called. *That's strange*, Clair reflected. She didn't usually think of Sadie as an old woman. She had gotten in the habit of calling her friend every day on the days they didn't work together at the bakery.

Her thoughts came back to the present in a rush. She could hear Sophie howling. Her stomach knotted painfully. She knocked briefly at the door and pushed it open. Sadie lay on the floor, unconscious, with book boxes scattered all around her. Sophie sat guarding her mistress and continuing to howl her distress. Clair checked to see if Sadie was breathing, which she was, and called for an ambulance.

Sadie regained consciousness as the ambulance pulled into her driveway. She looked at Clair and moaned. Tears started running down her face and pooling in the wrinkles of her neck. The knot in Clair's stomach exploded and sent tremors throughout her body. She was shaking as Sadie was moved onto a stretcher.

Clair sat in the hard, oversized plastic chair next to Sadie's hospital bed. She called Tina and asked her to put the closed sign on the bakery. She also asked Tina to call Sadie's daughter in Philadelphia to ask her to check on Sophie. Sadie's right leg was broken in two places; it hung from a sling with pulleys attached to the bed frame. Sadie wasn't going to die, at least not today, but she was going to be out of action for a long time. Clair thought about what that would mean for the bakery and for her. But mostly she thought about what it would mean for Sadie. She pushed away the guilt that kept creeping around the edges of her thoughts. She knew those piles of books were a hazard. Tina had been complaining about them for months. Clair was unwilling to confront Sadie about the books and unwilling to simply take charge and do something about the boxes herself.

Sadie forced her eyes open and quickly closed them again. The scene was impressed on her consciousness. Her body was lying in a narrow hospital bed. Her right leg was pulled away from her torso at an uncomfortable angle and attached to ropes hanging from the bedframe. Her right arm was attached to plastic tubing connected to a plastic pouch hanging next to the bed. Her whole body ached, and she couldn't turn to either side. She was wearing one of those awful white hospital gowns with blue patterns printed all over it. She was covered in a rough white sheet and a white woven blanket.

She could feel Clair sitting next to her, but she felt more alone than she had ever felt in her life. She was so afraid, and she couldn't escape the fear. What if she would never be able to walk again? What if her heart couldn't take the strain? What if Clair gave up the bakery and there was no money coming in? What if she had to go into a nursing home? What if, what if? She was caught in a whirlpool of fears, each building off the other and spinning around her. She felt the sweat on her body. She was sticking to the sheets under her, and she couldn't escape where she was. She couldn't stop the groan.

"Sadie, are you Ok?"

"Of course I am not OK. Snake spite! I am squired through the leg and hanging from a hospital bed. How in creation could I be OK?"

"Sorry, that what a stupid question. Do you want a drink of water? Should I call the nurse?"

A nurse walked into the room as if scripted. She carried a syringe, which she inserted into the IV tubing.

"I am going to give you something for the pain. We will try to stay on top of it for the first few days." She adjusted the speed of the dripping in the tube. "Do you prefer to be called Mrs. Murphy or Sadie?" she asked as she straightened the sheet and blanket.

"I would prefer not to be here at all."

"I can certainly understand that, but I can't change that. What I can do is offer you something to eat. Are you hungry?"

"No."

"My name is Pam. Call me if you need anything." She pointed to a plastic box with a red button attached to the metal bed rail.

Sadie stood at the top of a hill. She was alone. She was so hot. The sweat ran down her face and into her eyes. She could feel it running down her sides and sticking her shirt to her skin. She was so tired. She was halfway. She knew that. She knew that she was halfway from where she started and halfway to where she was going. But both her destination and her point of departure were unclear. She couldn't stay where she was. She felt too tired to either turn around or move forward. She woke to the sunlight streaming through the window of her hospital room.

"The doctor said two weeks of traction and then several months in rehabilitation," Clair told Sadie's daughter, Hannah.

"Yes, I spoke with him yesterday. Clair, I can manage three weeks away; I am just not sure how I can help. I can't do much while she is in the hospital. I could get her house ready to sell, but she's having none of that."

"I know. We talk about it almost every day."

I had to admit that I was glad that my mother stayed on the island this past week. She not only helped out in the bakery, but she also spent time with Sadie in the hospital. Of course, her timing was excellent. It was an administrative week break for the university. They tried keeping Sophie with them, but she was worse than Molly. She would get out the doggie door and take off running, ears flying and snout to the ground. After the second recapture, Mom suggested that they ask Kat to keep her at the kennel. Kat was happy to help, and Sophie was moved to a safe, if not hound-approved, kennel.

I hated visiting my boss in the hospital. It wasn't just that I hated to see my old friend in pain; it was the whole unsettled situation. I knew how much Sadie hated being immobile. Medically, she was actually doing well, and her fractures were well aligned and healing. Mom said it was amazing that the breaks were so clean. When I first called her with the news, she feared that Sadie's old bones would have to be surgically replaced. According to the medical staff, she could possibly even get out of traction a few days earlier than originally planned.

Sadie was reading when I walked into her hospital room.

"Sorry I'm late," I said as I sat in the chair next to the bed.

"You know, your obsession with time is similar to mine with books," Sadie responded as she looked up from her book. "You think that if you could just control time, you could control your life. I think that if I could just gain enough knowledge from my books, I could control my life."

"But, Sadie, you have controlled your life. You built the bakery from nothing."

"No, Clair, control is an illusion. It is as much an illusion as time. Looking at a clock for you is like checking a label on a piece of clothing you want to buy. You already know you like the piece and you are going to buy it, or you wouldn't even bother to check the label. You always know what time it is, Clair."

"But I am always early or late."

"No, you're not. You just *feel* that you are. I have watched you for almost a year. You can do the accounts for a month past, plan the menu for two months ahead, order for the next week, and bake for the present day."

"But I always feel like I am out of time."

"That is exactly it, Clair. You *feel* like you are. But you are not out of time. You are out of balance, out of harmony, in your life. I think you have as much time as you need. I am beginning to think that we all do."

"Oh no, you've been talking to my mother, haven't you?"

Sadie laughed. "Well, she does help me to focus my thoughts. And she may be onto something with that synchronicity thing."

Sadie moved from the hospital into a nursing home on the southern part of the island. It was the only facility on the island that offered full rehabilitation services. Before Sadie could be released, she needed to rebuild her muscle strength and begin walking again. It would be a slow process, and Sadie was impatient.

March was a month out of time for me. My waking hours were divided between the bakery and Sadie. My mother came for a weekend and took Molly back with her. I was grateful. I didn't think I would miss the devil dog, but I did. Peter and Mom were keeping my head just above the water line. I didn't know if they actually planned it or if it just worked out that one of them was on the island every weekend. I was sure I would have drowned without their help.

Mom spent time with Sadie. She began clearing out the piles of books from the house and hired a cleaning service. Peter took me out for dinner, walks on the beach, and long nights of gentle loving. He was also helping me a little with Sadie's finances. I had been managing the bakery side of the finances, so I knew they were in good shape. Sadie long ago paid off the mortgage on the store. Even with taxes, business licenses, salaries, and supplies, the bakery made a good profit. Before Sadie broke her leg, Tina and I started to help organize her personal finances, but we didn't have a very good overall picture. All we did was give Sadie the bills she got in the mail and her personal checkbook. I wrote out the checks as I did for the bakery and Sadie signed them. Mom got permission from Sadie for me to handle the bakery finances. She also reluctantly allowed us to talk with her daughter, Hannah. The one thing she stubbornly refused to consider was moving out of her house.

It was the middle of April. The bakery was running at warp speed. We baked hot cross buns, monkey bread, and sugar cookies in the shapes of chicks and bunnies iced in pastel colors. Lunch offerings were tomato basil or split pea for soups and ham or egg salad for sandwiches. We sold out every day.

"We need extra help on Fridays." Tina said it every Friday.

"I know. I'll ask Sadie again."

I locked the door at the end of another long week. Tina and I sat at table four, but we weren't enjoying the splendid view out the window. We were wolfing down open-faced sandwiches hastily thrown together and cups of strong tea. We hoped that the food would give us the energy to clean up for the week.

"She can't go home, can she?" Tina asked.

"I don't think so. We would have to find someone to cook and clean and someone to walk Sophie," I replied.

"Well, I suppose we could find people to do that. But can she afford it?"

"I really don't know. She is just starting to talk to Mom about her personal finances."

"Do you think she'll sell the bakery?"

"I suppose she should consider it."

"Can you buy it?"

"No way. I couldn't even qualify for a loan to buy it," I confessed.

Tina sighed. "I don't know how I could make it without this job, and there isn't much else around Coupeville. Richard needs the truck to get to the dump, and I've got no transportation."

"I know. A lot of our lives depend on the decisions Sadie makes."

I compiled a list of possible assisted-living facilities with Shannon's help. It was a short list. As long as Sadie was making progress on her rehabilitation, Medicare would pay for the nursing home for a few months. Peter actually worked out an arrangement so that she could pay extra for a private room. It wasn't enough; even with a private room, Sadie hated it. Peter was infinitely patient with her.

Peter was on the island for the weekend. The kennel renovation was going well, and Josh's almost continual presence helped reassure him that his sister was safe. He approved a short list of potential managers that Kat and Marla would start interviewing next week. Naturally, he had Josh check out the applicants.

Peter pulled into the beach house late Friday night after an interminable wait for the ferry from the mainland. The sun had set. Josh sat on the front porch in the twilight, watching the moon on the bay. He heard Peter's car pull up but didn't move. Peter grabbed a beer and joined him.

"Yes, I checked on the girls. All is well in the dog domain."

"Any calls?" Peter asked.

"By any calls do you mean did Clair call? You know she didn't. Clair doesn't call."

Peter sighed. "I know. But wait, how do you know?"

"I pay attention."

"To Clair?" Peter's voice sounded strained.

"To everything. Don't go all territorial on me, pup."

"Sorry."

"Why don't you just go down there?"

"It's late. She's tired."

"Probably, but she's still waiting for you."

"You think so?"

"Like I said, I pay attention."

Peter walked down the beach to Clair's house. He didn't come back that night. Josh didn't expect him to.

The next morning, Peter made coffee while Clair made french toast.

"Did I tell you that Sadie never signed up for social security?"

"Are you sure, Clair? She has Medicare."

"Yes, she signed up for that and she has a supplement, as you know. She has always paid into social security for herself and anyone who worked for her, but she has never claimed a penny. She said it was just too complicated with her variable income from the bakery."

"Sadie's worked her whole life. That means if she retires from the bakery, she is probably eligible for a very nice income from social security."

"Peter, I don't think she has ever considered that."

"You told me that the bakery building is paid off. What about her house?"

"I have no idea. Would you go with me to visit her this afternoon?"

"Clair, I'm not sure that I am the one to talk to Sadie about her personal finances."

"Peter, I know she trusts you. She knows that you're the one who got her a private room."

Peter made a frustrated sound. "She won't even talk to her own daughter. What about your mother? Sadie is letting her clean out the house, right?"

"I hate to push this onto my mother."

"But you don't mind pushing it onto me?"

"Sorry, I guess I thought you wanted to help. My mistake." The hurt in Clair's voice was clear.

"No, I'm sorry, Clair. I do want to help."

Too late. Clair had pulled back into her shell.

She cleared the table before Peter even finished the food on his plate. Peter spent the rest of the weekend feeling guilty about his untimely response. The kennel was in great shape, almost complete. His sister appeared happy and relaxed, but Peter left the island feeling terrible. Clair wasn't answering his messages, and he was certain she was home on Saturday night when he knocked on her door. Her car was in the driveway, but no one came to the door.

Tasha brought Sadie some of the bakery's signature cinnamon rolls. She made two cups of tea in the common room and set up a tray. Sadie was sitting in her wheelchair, looking out the window of her room. Tasha set the tray with tea and rolls on a table and learned over to kiss Sadie on the cheek. She was the only one who dared to kiss or hug Sadie. Tasha's efforts were acknowledged with a small smile, and they drank their tea in a companionable silence.

"Sadie, why won't you consider moving in with your daughter?" Tasha gently asked.

"Don't want to be a burden."

"Staying here might be more of a burden for Hannah. Her job and her children are in Philadelphia. She worries about you, and there is little she can do to help from across the country."

"Don't need help. I just need to get out of this place." She would not look at Tasha.

"Sadie, be honest. You do need help."

When Sadie turned her face to Tasha, tears were rolling down her cheeks.

"I know I'm a stubborn old woman. I know I'm driving everyone crazy. I've lived on my own terms my whole life, and I just want to die that way."

Tasha took her hand. "And I want to help you. We all do, but you have got to be a little more flexible."

"She wants me to sell the house."

"Hannah?"

"Yeah. After her husband died, she started to renovate their carriage house into an independent apartment. Said she wanted it for me to live in. Thought maybe she was going to rent it out, but she didn't finish it."

Tasha let the silence just be. Sadie had to say this in her own way.

"Haven't seen it. Haven't been there for years. She needed some time for herself and the children after Don died."

"How long ago was that?"

"Six years or thereabouts."

They talked about Hannah and her children until someone came in to take Sadie to physical therapy.

CHAPTER 26

TASHA'S CLASSES WERE OVER by the end of May. She was close to completing her master's degree; she just had to take two classes over the summer and finish her thesis. She would need another full year of supervision to be eligible as a licensed counselor. Now she had to seriously think about finances. She got a wonderful break on tuition for being the daughter of a former dean, and she found a grant for the remaining fees. She had some savings left, but living expenses for a year without income were going to be a strain. She thought about asking Clair to let her rent out the upstairs apartment. It was small, but it would rent easily, and they could split the income. Her nursing license was current, and she always kept up to date on her continuing education credits, so she could always find a part-time job in nursing. She could always pay her own bills and buy food; self-sufficiency was vital to her.

It was Saturday afternoon, and she was sitting on the deck at the beach house. Clair was taking Sadie to visit one of the few options for assisted living on the island. Tasha knew it wasn't going to be acceptable. Sadie was fiercely independent, and both Tasha and Clair could identify with that. Sadie just hadn't counted on the inevitability of old age. Tasha was trying to help her be realistic and a little more accepting of this stage of her life. If she couldn't help Sadie, how could she help future clients? If she couldn't help Sadie, how could she help herself?

OK, enough introspection, she thought. *You need action.*

Tasha's self-talk took her to the garden shed where she armed herself with gloves and tools. She proceeded to a weed-covered bed on the side of the house. It was the traditional site for sweet peas. They were her mother's favorite flower, and Tasha planted them early each spring in her memory.

Josh found himself walking down the beach toward Clair's house. He knew Tasha was coming up sometime that weekend. He came up several times a week and most weekends to check the security system at the Bird Farm Kennels. He fell into an easy habit of staying at Kat's beach house, which Peter encouraged. The renovations on the property were almost complete. They would be finished sometime that summer, and then he would have less of an excuse to visit the island. The opportunities to see Tasha would also be less. *No, that is not going to happen.* The thought didn't surprise him, but the determination of it did.

Molly was a sandy, wet mess. This was not unusual, and it was one of the main reasons Tasha had several hoses with spray nozzles running from the front of the house to the lawn, which gradually slopped to the driftwood- and sand-covered beach of the bay. She grabbed Molly by the collar and began rinsing. Molly loved water and didn't unusually resist being rinsed off, but she broke away from Tasha and bounded back toward the beach. A distraction arrived in the form of a tall man who climbed effortlessly over the logs. As he reached the front lawn of the house, Tasha turned the water on him at full blast.

"Ah ha, another dirty dog that needs hosing!"

Josh walked toward her, undeterred by the soaking water or the barking dog.

He disarmed Tasha with ease and caught her with one arm around her waist, lifting her slightly off the ground. Molly circled them in noisy, ecstatic doggie delight.

Josh learned into Tasha and growled in her ear, "Where is Clair?"

"With Sadie."

"Ah."

"'Ah,' as in?"

"'Ah,' as in the coast is clear, and the shower and bedroom are free."

He nuzzled her neck, kissing her where it joined her shoulder. He breathed her in as though she smelled like perfume instead of wet dog and dirt. He set her on her feet. Tasha's legs felt like they would not support her. She leaned into him. The iron arm around her waist guided her toward the deck stairs. Molly realized they were through playing with her and took off again toward the beach in search of more diverting entertainment.

Sadie finally agreed, grudgingly, to visit the few independent- and assisted-living possibilities on the island.

Rose Hall was advertised as a small, home-like facility. It had a lovely setting with formal garden beds and cement walkways running between it. The old house in the center had two long wing additions on each side. Each resident had his or her own room and bathroom. They were obviously furnished with the residents' own belongings. We peeked into rooms with open doors that showed a variety of beds, chairs, tables, televisions, side tables, and décor. One room even had a large marmalade cat napping on the Afghan-covered bed. The hallways were broad and had railings, but they were unobtrusive. We looked at the one empty bedroom available. And then we were guided back to the main living area. Four residents were sitting around a card table. The room was comfortable and had a fireplace, a large screen television, and many recliners.

"Do you play bridge?" a resident named Mrs. Addison asked Sadie.

"No," Sadie snapped back.

"Well, I am sure that you could learn. We have a very active bridge club here."

"Not gonna happen," Sadie grumbled.

We moved down a short hall into the dining area. Four tables with matching chairs filled the room. Two ladies were arranging vases full of flowers on the tables.

"We dine family style." Mrs. Addison continued her tour monologue.

We stopped next to the second table.

"Polly, this is Sadie. She is thinking about joining us."

"Oh, lovely," the little blue-haired lady replied.

"I hope you are staying for tea. We have tea every afternoon. Oh, and book review on Wednesdays, music appreciation on Thursdays, current events week review on Friday, and movie night. Monday, of course, is health-check day."

"What, nothing on Tuesday?" Sadie asked mockingly.

"Oh, silly me. Tuesday is beauty salon," Polly answered. She either didn't catch Sadie's tone or chose to ignore it.

"Yeah, silly you, how could you forget beauty salon day—" I jumped in to cut off the rest of Sadie's comment. I knew where it was going, and it wasn't going to be pretty.

"Sounds like you keep very busy." My comment was not only an invitation to Polly, but also a warning to Sadie.

"Oh my, yes. We exercise every day. That's very important, you know. And the bridge tournaments, and we have outings, too—"

"It sounds lovely." I had to cut Polly off before Sadie exploded.

"Blue hair! They all had blue hair!" Sadie exploded as we pulled away from Rose Hall.

"Yes, I noticed. Beauty salon day is Tuesday." I replied with a calm voice that belied the acid churning in my stomach.

Sophie was not happy. She was in a kennel full of Doberman pinschers. She did not understand them. Oh, they spoke standard dog, but they were so full of energy and valiant intentions. They made her feel tired. They were all unfailingly polite to her, but this was not her home. Home was so close she could almost smell it. She had her own room, her own bed, and her favorite food at the kennel. Sometimes she got to spend time in the house. Quincy lived there. Bulldogs she understood. The people were kind, they petted her and spoke softly, but she missed her own human, and she wanted to go home.

The rain stopped, and there was a light breeze from the bay. Kat let Sophie out into the exercise yard with three of the older females. Sophie followed the other dogs around the fence line, reading messages and leaving a few, but she didn't join in the Doberman chase games. She stayed by the farthest edge of the fence and raised her snout to smell the breeze. Home. She smelled home and began to dig.

"Clair, it's Kat. Sophie is missing! She dug her way out under the fence. I'm not sure how long she has been gone."

"I'm sure she is headed home."

"Yup, that's my guess too. I am going there now."

"OK, I'll meet you there."

Kat walked around Sadie's house twice. The hound was not there. It started to rain again as she walked into the big field that eventually joined the kennel property. She heard Clair's car pull up into Sadie's driveway and changed directions.

"I was so sure she would be here, Clair. I am so sorry."

"I'm the one who should be sorry. I know what a beast Sophie can be; that's why I couldn't keep her at the beach. Have you looked in the woods behind the house?"

"No, I checked all around the house and the garage. She is not here, and I just started to look in the field," Kat responded.

"I think we would see her if she were in the field. Let's look in the woods." I noticed that Kat was alone. "Where's Cerberus?"

"Well, Sophie is not a big Doberman pincher fan, so I left him at home."

"Sophie is a spoiled beast. I brought some cheddar cheese; it's her favorite treat."

They were ten minutes into the woods when something awful hit them.

"What is that smell?"

"I don't know, but it is terrible, isn't it? Hey, isn't this the area near Chief Snakelum's gravesite?"

"I think it is."

They broke into a clearing.

The gravesite was covered in garbage. The chain-link fence was cut and torn in several places, and dead animal bodies hung from the top of the fence. Sophie was outside the fenced area, rolling in a pile of something brown. The smell was beyond nauseating.

"Ah…who would do this?"

"It looks like someone dropped a whole dumpster of garbage."

"Yeah, and then collected road kill for a finishing touch."

Kat learned down and snapped a leash on Sophie's collar. "Bath time for you, bad, old hound girl."

They alternately coaxed and dragged the recalcitrant basset hound back to the cars.

"I'll take her, Kat," I offered.

"No, we are all set up for dog baths. Don't worry. I'll keep her in the house from now on. She likes Quincy. No more escapes for you, my girl."

"But what will Marla say?"

"She'll be fine with it. You have your hands full with the bakery and Sadie. How is she doing, by the way?

"Physically, her recovery is amazing."

"I hear a 'but.'"

"You are right. But I can't find an acceptable place for her to live after the rehabilitation."

Josh called Peter before it hit the newspapers.

"What the hell? Why didn't Kat call me?" Peter demanded.

"Because she knew you would act like a jackass. I've been up there. It's the same thing that happened to Sadie's house in the fall," Josh replied.

"What is that stupid sheriff doing about it?"

"Not much he can do if he can't catch the vandals in the act, and they are too sporadic for that."

"Why is it all in the same area?"

"Good question. I thought it might be about devaluing

the property around the Bird Farm, but that seems unlikely since Kat set up the kennel."

"Should I go up?"

"No. I'm going back up this afternoon. I've moved up the installation of the perimeter security system even though the exterior renovations aren't complete."

"Should I bring Kat down here?"

"I doubt you could do that. Kat may be fragile, but she has claws. I'll stay on the island until this is resolved. I have some ideas. We may need to set some bait."

"You are *not* going to involve my sister in some wild paramilitary operation!"

"See what I mean by jackass response, Peter? I'm going to finish up here in the office, and I'll be back on the island by tonight."

"Call me. I want regular reports."

"Copy that."

It took all of Peter's willpower not to call his sister. He rescheduled his appointments for Friday and left for the island late Thursday evening. He arrived close to midnight, but Josh was still up.

"You are certain the girls are safe?"

"That is the second time you have asked me that. Yes. These clowns are not going to make another move right now. They are going to wait and see what desecrating the chief's grave does for them. And yes, the kennel is well secured. I've been spending a lot of time there."

"I know, Josh. I'm just worried."

"Will you be spending the night with Clair?" Josh asked.

"I made a stupid remark, and she won't forget it or forgive me for it. I swear she has a memory like a steel trap."

"All women do. Memories like elephants. It's genetic. You have to—"

"I know. Pay attention." Peter cut him off.

Josh returned to the local paper.

"OK, scumbag. Got ya!"

"What?"

Josh handed Peter the paper.

The ad was a small one in the general real estate section.

"Wanted: land on North Whidbey Island."

"Call Clair. We need a strategy session."

They met in Sadie's room at the nursing home. Josh outlined the plan.

"Sadie, you don't have to do this," Tasha said for the third time.

"Hell yes. I want to do it!" Sadie answered enthusiastically.

"I still think I should be the one to make the call," Tasha said. "I am a better actress than Clair."

"No, I'm the natural one to make the call."

"Make the call, Clair," Josh ordered.

"Hi, I'm calling about your ad in the paper—the one about land for sale." Clair didn't have to fake a nervous tone in her voice. "I mean I don't have land, but a friend of mine does…she might want to sell; there is a house too."

She listened for a minute. The phone was on speaker,

and everyone in the room was holding their breath, except Josh. He was breathing deep and easy.

Clair glanced down at the script. "She's in a nursing home right now." Pause. "Could you come and talk to her?"

She listened again and made a note.

"Yes, I think that will be OK. She is in Pleasant Manor. Do you know where that is?"

She made another note and hung up the phone.

"He's coming Monday afternoon at two o'clock." Clair made the statement just to be certain they were now going to proceed.

Everyone in the room exhaled at once.

"Hot damn!" Sadie exploded. "We've got the rodent cornered now!"

Monday Josh set up a device in Sadie's room. Clair refused to leave her side. Josh, Peter, and Tasha waited in Peter's car a block away from the nursing home. They could hear everything that was going on. Sadie was a star.

"I thought maybe we could make a kind of deal. You know, if I didn't have to pay a real estate fee, I could maybe make a little more money." Her voice was low and quivered just slightly.

"Yes, ma'am. I can certainly help you out. I'll just draw up the papers."

Thomas Bohan's manner was smooth and slick.

"I don't have a lawyer," Sadie ventured.

"No need, no need." He smiled. "We can just handle this between the two of us. I've worked in real estate for a long time. Let me look over the property and draw up the paperwork. I can be back to you early next week. Will that be OK?"

"Oh yes, that would be fine. I want to get this all settled before my daughter comes from Philadelphia. She doesn't think I can handle my own affairs anymore."

The ad was a big risk, but he was getting desperate. Hospital Corporation was closing the bids soon. The bird farm property was a big mistake. The old man behind the farm wouldn't sell, and that stupid family didn't have the sense to clear out after their well was fouled. But now the old lady broke her leg, and she was desperate. If there was anything Thomas Bohan loved, it was desperation—other people's desperation. Here was his chance; he just needed one domino to fall, and the whole thing would collapse his way. One more little push, and he was good at pushing.

OK, slime time. Make your move.

Josh knew that Bohan would make another attempt at intimidating Sadie and, thus, finalizing the sale; he was so desperate to make. It would have to be at her house. He knew it was empty with Sadie at the nursing home.

The trap was set, and he was more than ready to spring it.

CHAPTER 27

ZACH'S HANDS WERE SHAKING. This was wrong, so wrong. Travis poured a line of gasoline around the garage. Zach was supposed to be making a pile of kindling and then starting the fire. He knew the old lady wasn't in the house because he checked. Her dog was gone too. And he knew that the garage was empty. Dumping garbage and road kill was one thing, but setting fires…

"What's your problem, man? Why do I not see fireworks?"

"Ah, Travis I…I…"

"You got a stuttering problem on top of your no-guts issue? You are one lame dude."

Zach stood up on shaky legs and faced Travis.

"I quit."

"Get the hell away from me before I beat the shit out of you."

Zach turned and started to run.

"Show time," Josh said into the phone.

Just as Travis dropped a match in a pool of gas, two sheriff cars pulled up. Fire response was a few minutes behind. The ground was damp, and the garage was only slightly scorched. The house didn't catch at all. Josh waited to see that the authorities had things well in hand before he melted into the woods. After about thirty minutes, he walked casually into the field next to the kennel property.

"Very smooth operation, ghost rider." Tasha opened the door and let Josh into her university district apartment.

"Thank you, my lady. Do I get a trophy?"

"Nope."

"A badge, a token?"

"Hmm?" Tasha tilted her head up to look at him as if considering his request. "How about a kiss?" she asked as she went up on her toes and draped her arms around his neck. She kissed him lightly.

"How about more?" Josh growled as he pulled her closer.

"You are so greedy," she answered as he nibbled on her earlobe.

"Yeah, we hero types need a lot of action."

She pulled back from him a little. "I was worried about you, Josh. Is it routine business practice for security agencies to set up bad guys?"

Josh loosened his arms around her.

"Oh, Bohan's not a real bad guy. He's just a minor league goon."

"That doesn't answer my question. Are you always on a quest to seek out evil and right the wrong?"

"Well, it's not standard procedure, but this one just kind of fell into my lap. And speaking of my lap, could we get back to my reward?" He pulled her back up against him.

Tasha was up and in the kitchen before Josh. That was unusual. Maybe she was going to cook him a big breakfast. He liked to watch her in the kitchen. Hell, he liked to watch her, period.

"You may have been right," she said, placing a cup of coffee on the table in front of him.

"What? I can't be hearing clearly. I *might* have been right? About what in particular? What are you fixing for breakfast?" He didn't see any food out on the counter, and she wasn't heading toward the refrigerator.

"Don't get cocky. I'm still not certain about this."

"About what exactly?"

"Remember when you said we should live together?" She moved to stand next to his chair.

"I refuse to recall that remark on the grounds that I may incriminate myself."

"Cute. You could just tell me that you've changed your mind." She started to move away, but he grabbed her by the wrist.

"Wait, Tasha, I didn't say I had changed my mind. I was just playing."

"I'm not in the playing mood, Josh."

"Damn, Tasha. I was just caught up in the snappy verbal repartee. Come here, woman." He caught her hand and pulled her down into his lap. "You want to seriously consider living together?"

"I like being with you," she said in a soft voice.

"Me too," he answered.

"I can't imagine being with anyone else."

"That's good. I feel the same way."

She pulled herself out of his lap and stood up. "I just wanted you to know that I am considering it."

Josh blew out an exasperated breath.

"I think I've mentioned to you that I am not into relationship drama," Josh said. Tasha moved out of his lap and walked to the door.

She turned, looked hard at him, and walked out of the room.

Oh, very smooth, pal, Josh thought to himself. He didn't slam the front door on his way out, but he did slam his car door.

I tried to be relieved that the Bohan operation went so well; everyone else was. I was too worried about Sadie to be satisfied with the status quo. This was the last facility on the list. Sadie had only two weeks left at Pleasant Manor. As usual, time and I were at war.

The living areas of the facility were divided into three separate buildings called pods. Patients, or residents, as the administration preferred to call them, were grouped by mental acuity and physical mobility. Sadie hated the place instantly.

By the time we worked our way through the third pod, I could barely keep Sadie in the wheelchair.

"Great drooling dinosaurs, its zombie land! Get me the hell out of here!"

"But you haven't seen the dining areas or the common areas for socialization," their administrator tour guide protested.

"Possibly another time," Clair murmured as she turned Sadie's wheelchair toward the exit.

They passed an elderly gentleman moving at a fast pace. He had on a white button-up shirt and a tweed jacket. He had nothing on below the waist. A harassed-looking aide was close on his heels.

"Mr. Johnson, you must put your pants on."

"Nope!" He passed them at a trot, winking at Clair.

"Never! Never! Never!" Sadie expounded in a loud voice.

The facility was clean and appeared to be adequately staffed, but Clair had to agree with Sadie that it was horribly depressing. She could not see her old friend living in zombie land.

Peter was back on the island. He and Clair were talking again after the successful real estate drama.

"Peter, please talk to Sadie. We have seen every assisted-living facility on the island. She won't accept any of them."

"What does your mother say?"

"If she's talking to Sadie, Mom's not telling me. She did bring her some paperwork from the house, and Sadie asked her to get some things from her bank box."

"She let Tasha get papers out of the bank?"

"Yes, but she still won't talk to us about the house."

"What about the bakery?"

"Oh, just crazy talk. She wants me to buy the bakery from her."

"Clair, that's a great idea."

"Peter, I can't buy the bakery. I can barely pay my electric bills in the winter. "

"You are exaggerating. Sadie could carry the mortgage, and we could structure a payment plan so that she has a steady income while you build up equity in the bakery."

Peter's eyes were sparkling, but I was just angry.

"Are you in a time warp? I would never qualify for a loan, not even a loan for the down payment."

"I'll loan you the down payment."

"No way!"

"Clair, it's perfect. Sadie doesn't need a big lump sum of money, especially not if she sells her house. She would be better off with payments on a regular basis."

"How would you know what Sadie needs? You won't even talk to her."

"Don't be so stubborn, Clair. Sadie knows exactly what she wants, and she told you."

I could feel my voice getting louder. "Stubborn? I'm stubborn? You won't even talk to her."

"All right, all right. I'll talk to her."

"Go away, Peter."

"What?"

"Go away. I'm angry with you, and I'm going to stay that way awhile. You need to be in another time zone."

⁓

"You called her stubborn?" Josh asked in disbelief.

"I know, I know, bad call. But I'm just so exasperated with her."

"Exasperation is the normal state of affairs when you are dealing with women."

"What the hell am I supposed to do? I finally got my sister settled. I got Sadie's finances straightened out, and Clair is just…unmanageable!"

Josh looked at Peter and raised one eyebrow.

"You can't manage Clair, Peter. And things are never settled."

"I've been paying attention. I swear. I am just so frustrated."

"Cold showers help on a short-term basis."

"Very helpful!"

"Keep paying attention, and an opening will come up. You just have to be ready."

"You sound like Clair. It's all in the timing."

"It's all the same thing. Call it paying attention, call it timing, or call it synchronicity."

"Speaking of Tasha, I don't think paying attention is helping you much there."

Josh smiled. "Well, Tasha is a challenge. I may have lost my focus for a few minutes. Like I said, cold showers help a little."

Sadie moved out of the nursing home and back into her house. I was spending the night and Sadie's daughter, Hannah, was arriving the next day. The Bohan affair seemed to energize Sadie, and she spent several hours with Peter reviewing her personal finances—not that either one of them talked to me about those sessions.

I parked the car as close to the house as possible and got Sadie's walker out of the trunk. Sadie got out of the car and stood for a long minute looking at her house. She grunted. "Strange. Don't feel a thing."

"You mean you can't feel your leg?"

"No, silly, course I can feel my leg. Aches like the devil. I mean I don't feel a thing about the house. Don't love it, don't hate it; it's just a building."

We moved into the kitchen, and Sadie sat at the table.

"Tina is bringing over an early dinner," I said.

"Yeah, you told me. I still have my short-term memory."

"Sorry," I muttered. "I'll just bring in your things from the car."

The three of us sat down to a dinner of meatloaf, mashed potatoes, peas, salad, and rolls and peach cobbler from the bakery.

"I don't know how to thank you for the car, Sadie, especially after what that fool son of mine did," Tina said.

Sadie signed over her three-year-old Subaru station wagon free and clear to Tina the week before she moved out of the nursing home. It was one of the things she and Peter worked out without me.

"I've got no use for the car. You and Clair have kept the bakery going this past year. I owe you."

Dinner was finished. Tina started to clear the table.

"Thanks for dinner, Tina. It was great," I said.

"Yeah, it was," Sadie asserted.

"Sadie, do you want to take a short nap? Peter is not bringing Sophie home until later this evening."

"I think a nap would be timely, Clair," Sadie answered with a smile.

Sadie got settled into her bed while Tina and I proceeded to clean up the kitchen.

"Well, her appetite is good," I said.

"Yes, and she can get around really well with her walker. She just tires easily."

"How long is her daughter staying?"

"Two weeks. You know, Sadie's agreed to move back with her."

"Is she going to sell the house?"

"Yes, can you believe it?"

"What about the bakery?"

"I don't know. She and Peter have some ideas. I think they want to talk to Hannah first."

"Tina, how is Zach doing?"

"Well, he cooperated fully with the police after Travis ratted him and that Bohan jerk out. Turns out Travis dumped a dead cat in our well. He was working for Bohan way before Zach got involved."

"So, what will happen to Zach?"

"They moved him yesterday from the jail to across the mountains at that 'Tough Guy' program. It's for a year. I think it's kind of like a boot camp mixed with survival stuff. It's real hard, but there is a waiting list for it. I didn't think we could get him in. It was so lucky that my son, Joe, the one that's in the army, was home on leave. He set it up. I think that Josh fellow had something to do with it too. I'm grateful. Troubled as Zach is, I hate to think of him in prison."

"I'm so glad that things worked out for your family, Tina."

"Yeah, things have been pretty bad this last year, but it does look like it's all working out now."

Tina left, and I brought my overnight stuff in from the car. I planned to sleep on the couch in the front room. I didn't want to be in one of the bedrooms upstairs if Sadie needed me during the night. Peter brought Sophie over at about 7:30 p.m. Sadie and her hound were joyfully reunited. Peter declined my offer for dinner, kissed Sadie on the cheek, and left.

Tasha met Hannah at the airport, and they drove to the island.

"I can't believe that my mother has finally agreed to move!"

"Well, it hasn't been an easy transition for her."

"I brought the floor plans and pictures of the carriage house. I thought she might like the idea of finishing it off herself. "

"That's a good idea. It is hard for her to give up her independence."

"I don't want to take her independence. I just want to help her."

"I know. Are you prepared for the hound from hell? You know, that is part of the deal."

"Oh yes. I had a guaranteed hound-proof fence installed in the yard behind the carriage house and a doggie door in the kitchen."

"Good moves."

"I can never thank you and Clair enough for all you have done. I feel so guilty about not coming earlier."

"Don't waste your energy on guilt. I think things have worked out exactly as they were they were supposed to. And I firmly believe that both old hounds are capable of learning new tricks."

Hannah's stay was a two-week whirlwind. I wanted to close the bakery and help, but both Sadie and Hannah were totally opposed to that idea. It was May, and the lilacs mixed with the sea smell and perfumed the air. Iris called to see when I was coming back to work in the nursery. It was the second time she called. I told her I just couldn't make time for it right now. Mom had a light schedule with summer classes only twice a week. She came up for a few days and helped Sadie pack things. Hannah said they could hire a moving company for half a load, but Sadie managed to get everything she wanted to take in boxes. Most of the furniture went to the bargain barn. Tina was bringing them dinner almost every night. She was so grateful to Sadie for the car.

It turned out that the house *was* paid off.

Sadie put it up for sale without any remorse. Marla and Kat were making all the arrangements to ship Sophie back. Marla shipped dogs all over the world. The weather conditions were going to be good for Sophie to fly on the same flight as Sadie and Hannah. Hannah's children would meet them at the airport. Mom was in charge of mailing Sadie's boxes. She left the island without seeing Josh.

I felt like everyone was helping but me. By the second week, plans were moving along in an amazingly timely manner. On Monday, the bakery was closed, and Tina had the supply delivery covered. She was working fulltime now. I called Hannah and told her I was bringing over lunch. It hit me hard to see the For Sale sign in the yard. Inside, the house was almost empty. It finally dawned on me that Sadie's time on the island was truly coming to an end.

Hannah, Sadie, and I sat in Sadie's kitchen.

"Clair, I want you to buy the bakery. I don't care about the money." Sadie would not break eye contact with me.

"This is what I want too, Clair." Hannah's voice was soft but firm. "We could do this long distance, but it would be so much easier to finish it now. You know that Peter has all the paperwork drawn up."

"What about putting the bakery up for sale?"

"Don't want the hassle," Sadie snapped

"You could probably get a better price for it."

"Don't care! It's my bakery, and I want you to have it!"

"Don't you want it, Clair?" Hannah asked.

"I…" My breath caught in my throat. "Yes, I love the

bakery. I love working there. I'm just not certain about owning it.'"

"Well, time's running out. The bakery closes in a week if you don't buy it." Sadie pulled her walker toward her and marched out of the kitchen.

"At least take a look at the agreement." Hannah handed me a file.

"Sadie and Peter have already signed this," I said in a weak voice.

"Yes, all it needs is your notarized signature."

I rarely called my mother for advice. I was feeling desperate.

"Mom, what am I going to do about the bakery?"

"Clair, someone recently told me that opportunities missed are opportunities gone. They never return."

"I hate the idea of taking advantage of Sadie because of the timing."

"I don't think either Sadie or Hannah feels that way. Sometimes, we need to accept things that are offered with gratitude. I think that's what Sadie needs from you right now."

"But what about Peter? How can I borrow the money from him?"

"Do you really think that Peter would take advantage of you?"

"You always preached independence."

"Yes, and here's your chance for it. Clair, think it over, make your decision, and move on."

"You mean 'time's a-wastin'?"

CHAPTER 28

ON TUESDAY MORNING, PETER stopped into the bakery. Tina was loading the dishwasher. I was just unlocking the door. I backed away from the door as he entered.

"Clair, let me lend you the money to buy the bakery."

"We've had this discussion, Peter. I am not going to borrow money from you."

"It's a good investment. Venture capital is one of the things I do. I've reviewed all the records, and I will make money on the deal."

"No, you won't. The interest rate you want to charge me is ridiculously low. In fact, the price of the bakery is ridiculously low."

"That was Sadie's decision. She is making back what she invested plus a nice profit," he said.

"But you know that she could sell it for more," I insisted.

"She probably could, but she wants things settled quickly, and she wants you to have it. The house may be on the market for a while since it is neither waterfront nor view property."

"I thought she was considering renting the house."

"She is if she can find someone to manage it for her, but she doesn't really need the income. You know, Hannah wants you to have the bakery too."

"I just feel like I am taking advantage of Sadie and Hannah and you."

"Clair, you are *not* taking advantage of anyone. This is what good timing feels like."

"You mean good timing for *me*!"

"Good timing for everyone, if you're not too stubborn to take the opportunity."

Peter's exit was somewhat less than theatrical because he got halfway up the steps and had to turn around. He forgot to purchase the cinnamon rolls he promised Josh.

Peter walked into the beach house and dropped the box of rolls on the kitchen counter.

"Looks like you are armed and dangerous."

"She's had enough time. I'm not waiting for a chance any longer. I am making my own chances."

"There speaks the CEO of a multimillion-dollar corporation. Well, there is something to be said about taking your advisory unaware. Go get her, tiger."

There were no lights on in Clair's house that night. Even the porch light was off, but the full moon gave Peter all the light he needed. He pounded on her front door. He might have been happy that the neighbors were off island if he thought about it. But he wasn't thinking about it.

What was that banging? Molly was sleeping soundly in her bed. Did Sadie have a relapse? Was there an emergency at the kennel? Was the bakery on fire? All manner of catastrophes raced through my mind as I opened the front door. Peter stood there, looking like an archangel with the moonlight shining on him. I had a moment to consider how I must look. I was wearing green pajama pants with purple Eeyores. They were cut off raggedly above my ankles because they were just sleeping pants, and I hadn't bothered to hem them. On top, I had on an old blue sleeveless tank with faded orange writing, which once belonged to my brother. I couldn't remember whether I washed my face or brushed my teeth before falling into bed, and I knew my hair was a tangled mess. I pushed it out of my eyes and snapped on the porch light.

"Where's your guard dog?"

"Sound asleep in her bed."

"Great security system."

"Stop right there. Don't you worry about my safety or security. You are not responsible for me, Peter Cameron. And—"

Peter stopped whatever else I planned to say by stepping inside the doorway, causing me to back up. He put his hands on my shoulders. From the look on his face, I thought he was going to shake me.

"Clair, stop! Pay attention. I love you."

"What?" I couldn't have heard him right.

"I love you, Clair. I want to marry you."

"No. No you don't. You just feel responsible for me."

He tightened his hands on my shoulders.

"I don't need to be responsible for you, Clair. You can do that for yourself. I want to see what outrageous outfits you are going to wear every day." I started to sputter at that. Peter put one finger gently on my lips. "I want to watch you toss the hair out of your eyes. I want to laugh while you chase Molly down the beach or when you close your eyes taking a soufflé out of the oven. I want to hold you as you fall asleep in my arms. I want to walk into a room with you and see all the clocks reset themselves. Share your magic with me, Clair. Marry me."

I couldn't think of a single word to say. Peter pushed the hair out of my eyes and kissed me very lightly on my lips. He took my hand and pulled me toward the bedroom.

I had to admit, the timing was perfect. Peter and I drove Sadie and Hannah to the airport. Kat and Marla delivered Sophie to air cargo at zero dark thirty. I agreed to spend the night at Peter's apartment.

I woke suddenly. My heart was pounding. I knew even before I opened my eyes that I was not in my own bedroom, not at the apartment or at the beach. What time was it? Where was I supposed to be? The dream was still in my head as reality. Timers were going off all around the bakery, buzzing, ringing, and screaming. The air was full of smoke and the smell of burnt chocolate cake.

Peter came out of the bathroom, his hair wet from the shower.

I was in a panic.

"Peter, I can't borrow money from you for the bakery. You know how bad my timing is. What if next year I decide I don't want to manage a bakery?"

"Sweetheart, the bakery is a done deal. If you hate it in a year, then we'll sell it at a profit, buy milk goats, and learn to make cheese." He sat on the edge of the bed.

"How did you know about the milk goats? Did Tasha tell you that was one of my wild dream schemes?"

"No, I'm just paying attention."

"What?"

"You ordered several books on the subject from the library. I noticed them on your bedside table."

"Are you always going to be one step ahead of me?"

"No, I'm working on making our timing fit together flawlessly."

He learned over and kissed me, and it was perfect timing.

CHAPTER 29

IT WAS ONLY EIGHT o'clock in the evening, but Tasha decided that she was going to bed early. She had been pushing herself the past few months, and she needed rest. She was going to reach her goal. By the end of the summer, she would have her master's and be well on her way to becoming a licensed counselor. The psychologist she was working with was impressed with her, and she already had some prospective job offers. Now she wasn't sure what was next. She wasn't certain that she wanted the responsibility of guiding other people's lives. Look how long it took her to straighten out her own life. Maybe this isn't where she needed to go. She took a deep breath, trying to center herself and stay calm. Doubt was just another fear.

She couldn't sleep. She knew better than to just lie there and ruminate. All right, up then—she did a tai chi routine and meditated.

She was watching *Firefly* reruns when Josh knocked on

her front door.

He was holding a quart of Chunky Monkey ice cream and a huge bouquet of white tulips with delicate green ferns. He stayed away for almost a month.

Tasha knew who it was before she answered the door. What she didn't know was how she felt about seeing him. She backed away from the door to let him in.

"What, no guard dog?" He extended the flowers toward her.

"Fast asleep on my bed," she answered, accepting the offering.

"*Firefly?*" he asked, tilting his head toward the sound coming from the television. Tasha nodded.

"I love that show. I can't understand why they canceled it. It was one of the very few that was worth anything," He started to walk toward the small room where Tasha kept the mostly unused television set. Josh stopped and turned back toward her. "I don't see you as a science fiction buff."

"I love some science fiction. It's the perfect forum for exploring possibilities and existential angst."

"Terry Pratchett," he replied, acknowledging the quote.

Tasha took the flowers to the kitchen. She arranged them in an old silver pitcher and picked up two spoons.

Dropping down next to Josh, she handed him a spoon.

"You are problematic for me," she stated.

"How can that be? We both like Chunky Monkey and *Firefly*..."

"True. And you did remember that I love white-and-green flowers. How did you ever find Chunky Monkey in such a large size? I've only ever seen it in pints."

"I have amazing connections."

Josh removed the cover from the ice cream container, and there was contented silence between them.

The problem with late night TV, aside from the never-ending infomercials, was that even great shows looped back on themselves, and eventually, you were watching reruns of reruns. Tasha turned off the television and started to get up off the couch. Josh caught her hand.

"Tasha, I'm sorry. I was an ass. If you need to talk, I need to listen."

"I'm sorry too. I think I was dealing with demons from my past."

"Well, demons rarely give up. You need to know this if you're going to help people deal with their demons. They sneak back when you are not paying attention. And they take different forms at different times in your life."

"My hero."

"No one can fight your demons for you, my love. But if you let me, I sure as hell can cover your back while you're in battle."

Molly woke from a deep sleep with a joyful bark when she recognized Josh's scent. And she didn't put up a fuss when he ordered her off the bed and out of the room.

EPILOGUE

HANNAH WROTE TO CLAIR that Sadie and Sophie were settling well into their new home. Sadie was working two mornings a week in a literacy program at the library, teaching adults reading skills. She was also spoiling her family when she got the urge to bake.

www.ingramcontent.com/pod-product-compliance
Lightning Source LLC
LaVergne TN
LVHW010542160826
845677LV00013B/2965

* 9 7 9 8 9 8 6 5 6 8 5 7 7 *